DAHAN
(THE

Suchitra Bhattacharya

Translated by
Mahua Mitra

This book is given as part of World Book Night 2015 by Central Sussex College.

SRISHTI PUBLISHERS & DISTRIBUTORS
64-A, Adhchini
Sri Aurobindo Marg
New Delhi 110 017
srishtipublishers@forindia.com

Published by SRISHTI PUBLISHERS & DISTRIBUTORS 2001
Copyright © original title in
   Bengali *Dahan* with Suchitra Bhattacharya
Copyright © for the English translations
   SRISHTI PUBLISHERS & DISTRIBUTORS 2001

ISBN 81-87075-75-9
Rs. 195.00

Cover photograph courtesy:
Bijay and Kalpana Agarwal, Gee Pee Films Private Ltd

Cover Design by Arrt Creations
45 Nehru Apartment, Kalkaji, New Delhi 110 019
arrt@vsnl.com

Printed and bound in India by
Saurabh Print-O-Pack, Noida

All rights reserved. No part of this publication may
be reproduced, stored in a retrieval system, or transmitted,
in any form or by any means, electronic, mechanical,
photocopying, recording, or other wise,
without the prior written permission of the Publisher.

Contents

1.	Chapter one	1
2.	Chapter two	19
3.	Chapter three	37
4.	Chapter four	49
5.	Chapter five	61
6.	Chapter six	79
7.	Chapter seven	95
8.	Chapter eight	107
9.	Chapter nine	129
10.	Chapter ten	149
11.	Chapter eleven	163
12.	Chapter twelve	175

13.	Chapter thirteen	193
14.	Chapter fourteen	211
15.	Chapter fifteen	227
16.	Chapter sixteen	243
17.	Chapter seventeen	261

Chapter One

*T*heir bodies met head-on like waves coming together in a stormy sea. Waves mounting waves; an upsurge of primeval passion. The handsome youth moved in perfect harmony with the lyrics and the rhythm of the music; each thrust of his chest, back and pubis was pressing against the beautiful young woman wantonly. Three quarters of her body were bare – an ocean of bare skin lay between her choli and ghagra. Each curve in the waxy glow of her youthful body sparked off an electric passion.

Jhinuk looked away in disgust. The television was a new craze in the city, reigning over every household with its string of different channels – the first channel, the second channel – Star, Mand Zee, with variations of the same lurid scenes everywhere. Watching such scenes even a few years ago, one would get a taste of forbidden pleasure. Now they were commonplace; time travelled at lightning speed. Freedom was in the air. This was a free society, a liberal economy, with gratuitous entertainment and glossy advertisement adding colour and glitz to life.

Bishakha's father suddenly came into the room and switched the TV off. "How can you possibly stay glued to these song-and-dance programmes? Young people like you! The table's laid out. Come and help yourselves. Why don't you relax and have fun instead of sitting stiffly, staring into the screen ..."

"That's enough! Leave them alone." Bishakha's mother was visibly annoyed. "Except dreary people like you, everybody loves watching this programme. We'll get up as soon as it is over."

"It needn't be. You won't miss much if you don't watch that romp! I'd like to have dinner – come along."

Bishakha's sister – fresh out of school – and their cousin, a young boy in middle school were fond of the programme. The two adolescents fretted and fumed if the programme was stopped midway. Now, unable to express their anger, in the presence of their sister's friends, the duo marched stiffly out of the room.

Jhinuk, however, was inwardly pleased when the TV was switched off. It was not as if she never watched TV, but that was only at home.

It was a different experience then. Jhinuk would watch and weave a fantasy around those scenes. She would escape from reality – it felt as if there was no school; the endlessly sleepy afternoons did not exist; and the evenings, meandering on the road, among old, faceless people – had dissolved, become insubstantial. Life would then centre around the little world in the box. Their tiny 750 square feet flat at Chanditala, the six feet by three feet balcony opening to the south, the potted crotons – everything would be erased to create a sprawling, dazzling, luxurious palace! The magic box entered her bloodstream like a forbidden but irresistible addiction. Scenes from the screen took on real colours. And during those magic moments, Jhinuk would feel she was with Tunir– walking down the quiet forest paths, or immersed in ecstasy under the crystal clear waterfalls– she would feel Tunir's deep presence around her, momentarily forgetting he was not close by.

But the vulgarity on the screen was too much! Ugh!

Sulagna whispered to Bishakha as her parents left the room, "Please switch the TV on and turn the sound off. They might just air *Khalnayak's* songs today."

"They won't," said Mainak. "They've banned Sanjay's films. Let the hero be acquitted of the TADA (Terrorists and Disruptive Activities Act) charges first!"

Sulagna was almost in tears. She couldn't bear the thought of anyone in pain; be it an ant or an elephant. She was nicknamed *nazukdil* – the soft-hearted – by her friends.

"This is wrong ..." they exclaimed indignantly. "A young boy has made a mistake. He doesn't deserve to be treated in this manner ... It's cruel!"

"Ooh, poor baby! Stacking foreign arms at home to *play soldiers*, right?"

"Sh..h..h! it's not just him. What about the rest? I suppose your political leaders are fallen angels? Watch out for Rashid's case and see how he gets penalised!"

"Stop – will you? Dragging on a thoroughly boring topic!" Subhasis cut the discussion short. "Come along. Let's give Bishakha a toast to celebrate her new job with these chicken legs." Everybody picked up pieces of chicken from the plate. Jhinuk too, almost mechanically. Why wasn't Tunir there?

Mainak noticed Jhinuk's absentmindedness, her furtive glances towards the door. "Hey Srobona! Does Tunir have to lock up his office before he can leave?"

Jhinuk had been chewing bubblegum, like she always did, in moments of excitement or anxiety. It was almost a childhood habit. Sujata had tried her best but failed to put a stop to her daughter's bad habit. Chewing the gum hard, Jhinuk replied grimly, "Possibly."

Tunir was too involved with his office these days. The names of his colleagues Kuruvilla, Rajat Roy and of the finance director would creep into the briefest conversations he had with Jhinuk. He never left office before 7 or 7.30 in the evening, and cooked up excuses to go to work even on holidays.

Yet, Tunir was a different person before getting this job. He had lived like a man possessed; Jhinuk was in his dreams, his sleep, in his daily existence. Jhinuk, Jhinuk and – Jhinuk!

Even a day's absence from his beloved would cause a heartbreak. And social or family commitments were a dilemma.

"Jhinuk, you're off to Murshidabad for three whole days! I'll simply perish."

"You've a wedding to attend the day after tomorrow? I'll be waiting for you under the lamp-post across the road...Oh, bother!

I'm supposed to attend my uncle's funeral at Nabadwip – Well, no chance – I'll give it a slip. I shan't be able to return the same day. And who's going to take care of my funeral in that case?"

There were daily trysts with Jhinuk. But that didn't stop Tunir from writing long, soulful love notes, spilling over dozens of sheets of paper. Tunir had always been eccentric, working at extremes, never drawing the line – chaotic in his excesses. At times, Jhinuk would be completely at sea.

It seemed as if each of his eccentricities was carefully calculated; every move prompted by an intricate numbers game, ticking away deep in his mind. Before his chartered accountancy intermediate exam, Tunir had decided to spend nothing less than seven hundred and sixty-five hours studying. However, he didn't take his exams, as he had fallen behind his stipulated goal by thirty-one hours. And once, when he declared he would spend nothing less than one hundred and thirty-five hours a month with her, Tunir visited Jhinuk at unearthly hours, trying to make up for lost time, turning a deaf ear to her pleadings. He was almost like a child struggling to reach an impossible goal. Jhinuk had a hard time trying to explain Tunir's curious behaviour to her parents. Her mother was already inquisitive; even her father, who remained fairly unperturbed by major ups and downs in life, frowned upon Tunir's odd behaviour.

Has Tunir planned something similar about his work? Was he thinking of spending two thousand five hundred, possibly three thousand hours in his office so that he would be sent to the U.S.A.? He was crazy about that country!

Jhinuk spat the bubblegum out of the window. The air outside was still hot and humid. Was it because Bisakha's house was close to Jadubabu's bazaar that the room was stuffy? Jhinuk finally picked up a plate of food.

"Help yourselves to the chicken, please," urged Bishakha. "Tunir may never come, while Anindita and her husband have ditched us as well."

"Isn't Anindita expecting a baby?" asked Nilanjana.

Carefully rolling up pieces of paratha on his plate, Subhasis glanced at Bishakha out of the corner of his eye and said, "That would mean another treat for us."

"You're shameless!" Nilanjana rolled her eyes. "You haven't treated us to anything after you got a job – and you're already planning the next treat."

"Why are you getting angry? It's Anindita's husband who will have to treat us, not you."

"He won't. Money doesn't come easy."

"You make me laugh! He has simply to lay his fingers on his scalpel and money starts flowing in, smooth and fast. It's almost like ... um ... like ... hey Srobona, help me out. What is it like?"

"Well, it's like money flowing with just the swish of a pickpocket's razor," Jhinuk pursed up her lips and smiled.

"It's like the police stopping trucks for a bribe."

"I'm sure Anu's husband isn't one of those blood-sucking doctors! He attends the neighbourhood clinic for the poor, and charges them a nominal fee for operations."

"Anu has got *me* into trouble too, by not landing up," sulked

Jhinuk. "I have a couple of books to return which I had brought along. Have to lug them back now. Bother!"

Looking at Mainak, she asked, "Can you drop the books at Anu's, please? You live close to her place."

Mainak threw a glance at Bishakha. The two were deeply in love. Anindita had had a crush on Mainak while they were in college. He froze every time Anindita's name cropped up in Bishakha's presence.

"You can sit at home with those books," he advised Jhinuk. "Anindita will visit you soon. And if she doesn't, I'm sure her husband will."

"Why should they?"

"Because they will have to queue up at schools for their child's admission very soon."

"They needn't worry. Jhinuk, you can always fix up a last-minute admission for the child in your school. You surely have that influence."

Jhinuk laughed, "I definitely can't do that. There's no special quota for us teachers."

"You might not be having one, but I'm sure your headmistress does," retorted Nilanjana sharply. "You made good use of it yourself when you bagged the job."

Jhinuk had to suffer such taunts ever since she got the job. She had been a pupil of the school herself and had approached the Headmistress when the primary section-in-charge Gitali Basu informed her of a vacancy. With her post-graduation over, she was jobless. But Sunita Sengupta, the headmistress, had asked,

"Do you really want to teach seriously or is it a passing whim? You won't chuck it up without giving notice, will you?"

"Certainly not, unless I get a better offer," Jhinuk had replied.

"You better join a leave vacancy at present. Swapna will be away on maternity leave and you can take over her nursery section."

"And when she returns?"

" We'll see. We shall soon have to add a couple of sections to nursery as the number of new students is increasing," Sunita had said, her eyes gleaming. "The school's performance was excellent at the Board's school-leaving exams this year," she exulted. "Two of our students were among the Board's top rankers while about fourteen got star marks. Mr Sengupta too, wants former pupils of the school to join as teachers."

Nilay Sengupta, Sunita's husband, was a small-time businessman who also owned the school. He was far too busy to spare any thought for the school. Nevertheless, Sunita made sure she clubbed her husband's name with all school activities and administrative decisions – much like the marriage sign, the light streak of sindoor on the parting of her hair.

Jhinuk let off a sigh, "You don't realise how hard I have to work."

"Does a nursery school teacher really have to work? Teaching kids to draw mangoes and apples, practise the alphabets, sing nursery rhymes with them – 'Humpty dumpty sat on a wall' ... "

Jhinuk knew why Nilanjana was resentful. She had got first class marks at the university but her career since then had been pretty dismal. The pay, from her part-time job at an insignificant local college in Shyambazar, was a paltry hundred and twenty-five rupees a month. A door-to-door salesperson would perhaps earn more. But lucky Jhinuk had landed a job with twelve hundred a month!

Well, fair enough, if Nilanjana suffered from a complex of sorts, she perhaps had a reason for that. But didn't the school make sure that Jhinuk earned her pay the hard way? Babysitting about forty children for three whole hours! And those kids!

"Aunty, may I go to the toilet," cried one. "Aunty I'm wet," screamed another. "Aunty potty please!" yelled the third. And the rest were plain mischievous. They could sell their mothers down the street – Fighting, screaming little bullies! Those kids would start punching each other the moment they arrived, using satchels and rulers as weapons – each one a small Tipu Sultan* of the telly! They pinched, bit each other and scuffled with all their might.

The newest batch of kids were three-year olds, barely out of their diapers and feeding bottles. Homesick and miserable, they bawled for their mothers all day long. Today, a little girl was crying in the sharp notes of raga Lalit ... "I want my Ma..a.a.."

As if Jhinuk wasn't getting enough from this thankless job – dragging on with the nursery section for over a year, with no promise of ever graduating to the senior school.

She too was at fault. She was lazy and careless, not bothering to collect application forms for the teachers' training course. And

---

*Tipu Sultan, the ruler of Mysore, faught the British to save his kingdom. A TV serial, based on his life, was very popular in the 90's.

the maths paper at the administrative services exam had been a disaster.

No more afternoon naps, she decided. She would practise her arithmetic instead. Jhinuk lay half reclined on the couch. No use pouring her heart out to Nilanjana. They were all going through the same ordeal – birth pangs at the dawn of their careers.

Nobody wants to trail behind someone who had never scored high marks in the University exams! Jhinuk changed the topic to take Nilanjana's mind away from her hidden jealousies to more pleasant and congenial subjects. "Nilu, wasn't there another marriage proposal for you? Any progress?"

Nilanjana's face lit up. "The boy is arriving from Boston very soon," she said with a smile. "His mother and sister visited us last Sunday."

"Was there an interview? Did they check your handwriting like the previous people?"

"No! Apparently, the boy seems to have liked my picture. They just asked me routine questions. Did I plan to be a research scholar? What can I cook? Can I drive and can I keep house? One doesn't get domestic help abroad! The boy wants to choose his girl carefully. And then get married and take her back to Boston with him."

Jhinuk rolled her eyes. "Don't you be lenient this time. Interview the Boston guy properly. Ask him whether he can clean, dust, do the dishes, cook lunch and change nappies."

Subhasis was washing his hands in a glass of water near the window. "Let me know before you have the interview," he called out. "I'll frame the questionnaire."

Sulagna rolled with laughter.

"Imagine the guy sitting demure, on his knees, while Nilu twirling imaginary moustaches throw a volley of questions at him:'Tell me, is your complexion really this rosy or have you used makeup ... some American cream that makes you appear fairer than you are? Should I rub your skin with cotton wool and spirit?'"

The air in the room was decidedly lighter now with the cheerful banter. Jhinuk didn't find much reason to laugh though. Laughing didn't make matters light for girls who still faced demeaning interviews, and several rejections by the prospective groom's family while wedding negotiations were on. How could the idea of a boy facing the same ignominy, for a change, be amusing?

"All said and done, however much you might make fun of non-resident Indians, they rule the Indian market now," chipped in Mainak. "Has the Boston fellow managed to get a green card for himself?"

"He has," nodded Nilanjana, turning her head like a proud hen. "He has been living abroad for quite a few years now. In fact, his mother was complaining that her son might settle down in the US and never return!"

"Well, he shouldn't, if he is intelligent. Students who are brilliant haven't much of a future in this country. What about your brother, Srobona? Does he plan to take the GRE after his engineering and go abroad to study?"

"How should I know?" Jhinuk curled her lips. "He is still in the third year. Isn't it too early to decide?"

"No, it's not. One should plan one's life and career well in advance." Subhasis sounded serious. "I know your brother well enough. A bright boy like him should have a clear ambition in life."

Jhinuk's mind rushed back to her childhood, to memories of the discrimination she had faced in her family. And her mind rebelled. Was her brother really brilliant in the true sense of the word? She remembered her mother stuffing her little brother with sweets and milk puddings, treacle and candy, while the tutor coached him at home. Their parents made sure that their son received the best nutrients for both body and brain. Life was pretty easy for boys in this country and parents strove to give them the best of everything. Just how relevant was the question of natural talent?

Jhinuk's brother Chhoton had been sent away to an expensive boarding school. His parents took special care to give him the best education possible. Chhoton's performance in school had always been good. He had passed all public exams with flying colours. That had paved his way to one of the best engineering colleges in the country.

So where exactly did success lie? Within the achiever? In the achievement and the opportunities that came his way? Or was it embedded in his ability to seize the right moment? Whatever be the truth, her brother's brilliance was hardly a surprise, she decided.

Damn! Such thoughts were depressing. Jhinuk shook her head. Tunir would never turn up today and that was depressing enough. He shouldn't have promised he would come – he'd better stay glued to his boss in that case, as long as he wished.

The heat was almost unbearable now. Sticky and uncomfortable, Jhinuk went up to the wash-basin and splashed cold water on her face and neck. She brushed her hair, trying to freshen up. When she got back home, she would wash once again.

An attractive girl, Jhinuk used little makeup; her soft, clear skin, and deep, lustrous eyes gave a natural glow to her face. A light touch of kajal, a small bindi, lipstick always did the trick.

Carefully pleating the dupatta across her hand-embroidered flared gujrati kameez, Jhinuk stepped out of the toilet and found herself face to face with Bishakha's mother.

"Aren't you getting married in a few months' time Srobona?" the lady asked.

"The dates haven't been fixed, Aunty ...," Jhinuk replied, embarrassed.

"Anindita will soon be a mother. You're getting married shortly. Nilanjana will too ... probably. But your friend here doesn't seem to care." Bishakha's mother was deeply concerned about her daughter's unplanned future. And Jhinuk caught a hint of anguish in her voice.

Mainak was still jobless. Bishakha's mother pinned little hope on him anyway, often complaining about the relationship. Jhinuk sensed what could follow and tried brushing the topic aside. "Bishakha has got a job," she made herself sound cheerful. "Perhaps now ... "

" Rubbish," Bishakha's mother sounded brusque. "Not having a job doesn't prevent her from getting married, does it? I could have found an excellent match for her. Why don't you girls discuss the problem with Bishakha and give her some sensible advice? You could ask her to pay more heed to what we say and stop thinking about that good-for-nothing fellow."

Jhinuk was aware that Bishakha was much too sensitive about Mainak. But interfering in their personal problems was the last thing she had in her mind. She managed to edge past the lady and return to the drawing room again.

"Will you leave now, or are you going to wait for Tunir?" Sulagna asked.

Jhinuk popped another bubblegum into her mouth. It was ten past eight. Tunir was certainly not coming today. Had she known, she would have gone and visited her grandmother at the old age home instead of coming to this party. She had missed a couple of her weekly Wednesday visits to her grandma's.

"Come, let's go," she called out to Sulagna.

"Wait a while. Tunir has just left his seat in his office," said Subhasis, closing his eyes and concentrating hard on an imaginary scene, pretending to foresee the future. "Oh, there he goes into the toilet ... Now he blows his nose ... He is standing next to the image of Lord Ganpathy Bappa behind the receptionist's desk ... He is muttering a short prayer. He's fishing out the bunch of keys from his pocket ... locking up all the rooms one by one ... "

Nilanjana broke into peals of laughter. "Rubbish!" she exclaimed. "Tunir's office would never have an image of Ganpathy Bappa. It's a British company."

Jhinuk chewed her gum hard, trying to soften her anger.

"I told you a while ago that Tunir has become a social recluse," she blurted out.

"You're fuming."

"No, I'm not. Why should I be angry? It's not worth it!"

"Come on, be a sport." Sulagna put her arm across Jhinuk's shoulders. "This is precisely the time to build up one's career. Don't you hear Anindita saying that her husband never returns from the nursing home before half past ten or eleven in the night? If you want a comfortable lifestyle and plan to enjoy the good things in life, mustn't you work doubly hard?"

"And, for whose pleasure?" Jhinuk questioned herself. For someone who left for work at the crack of dawn and came home late at night, the phrase 'a comfortable lifestyle' was a fallacy, almost ironical. And how did one define pleasure anyway? Someone who didn't have time for the simple joys of life; couldn't spare a moment to watch a squirrel hide a nut in the grass. Someone who never got to see the sparkle of a million stars riding on the waves of the Ganga, aflame in the afternoon sun – could he be happy? Happiness was not to be found in going around in a maze endlessly.

There was Jhinuk's father, Manas Sarkar, for instance. A simple, honest soul and a gentleman to the core, juggling himself between classes in college, the coaching classes that followed and the private tutorials. Churning out leaflets of model questions, working out 'how-to answers' and 'made-easies' for university students by the dozen, and wooing the publishers. Life was a huge maze for him – his existence a permanent state of frenzy. Could *he* be happy?

Jhinuk heaved a huge sigh. She was sure her father didn't quite enjoy being on the run. But he couldn't help it. Growing financial needs in the family and shooting prices forced him to be the money-making machine that he was.

Jhinuk for instance, had always wanted a wardrobe for herself and she had been given one, recently. Her mother's craving for a colour television had been duly fulfilled, and her brother Chhoton had been given a VCP that he had long been pining for. The instalment on their flat, as well as their education had to be paid for. From time to time their father helped out his brother's family too. Fortunately, Jhinuk's grandmother sought no help from her sons and lived on her own savings. Would Tunir too, in that case, turn into a perfect mill horse?

~

Mainak and Subhasis didn't stir. Nilajana too, lived close by and would probably sit talking for a while. Nobody, except Jhinuk and Sulagna, made any move to leave. Out on the road, they were struck by a sudden wave of heat – more stifling than the hot air back in the room. The sultry summer sky hung heavy with a sulphurous smell.

Sulagna pulled at Jhinuk. "There's going to be a storm. Let's take the Metro, it'll be quicker." Jhinuk hesitated. "What about taking a bus instead? It would reach us straight home."

"Are you crazy? You plan to take one of those crowded buses home! They're as hot as a furnace. Be a sport, let's take the

Metro. I shall get off at Rabindra Sarobar. And you can take a rickshaw home from Tollygunge station."

Jhinuk looked up again at the sky. A storm was certainly brewing. It was going to come soon.

Chapter Two

Romita stopped suddenly near a shop window in New Market and called out to Palash. He had walked a few steps ahead of his wife and was looking about for her.

"Come and look at this beautiful denim skirt," she waved.

With all its lights on, New Market dazzled in its evening dress. Shops lured customers with their display under the flattering neon lights in the show windows. The air was heavy with the heat from the powerful bulbs and the breath of the crowd.

Palash walked back to Romita and lit a cigarette. The denim skirt was enticingly displayed on a mannequin, its ends tightly pinned to highlight the contours of a woman's body.

Romita's face shone with excitement, "Isn't it exquisite?"

Palash, however, found nothing unique about the dress. He pulled at his cigarette and asked, "What's so special about it?"

"The cut is simply wonderful. And I love this particular shade of denim."

Palash tried his best to look interested but his effort showed. Sulking, Romita moved away from the shop window. "Want it?" lowering his voice Palash asked.

"Forget it. You don't like it. You might be an engineer but you don't have any taste." Anger made Romita's nostrils flare and her face flush. Palash smiled indulgently, "Come on darling, don't be upset. Go on – buy it."

Romita threw another glance at the skirt; she couldn't take her eyes off it. Curbing her intense longing, she said, "Let it go. What will your mother think!"

"As if Ma hasn't ever seen you in a skirt! You're wearing skirts and trousers in almost half the Manali photographs. Did Ma say anything about that?"

Romita didn't protest. Palash's mother had given snide smiles while leafing through their honeymoon photographs, with Romita in a wide range of Indian and western clothes. She was, in fact, quite modern in her outlook, it was only his father who ...

Romita would often wonder how this man, who now walked beside her through the brightly lit lanes of the market, had been a complete stranger six months earlier. It had never occurred to Romita that she could develop a close relationship with Palash's parents, his brother and sister-in-law. How strange are the lives of women – a slight familiarity, a marriage, a few months of living together changed their entire world. Now, every moment, she was conscious of Palash's likes and dislikes, his family's as well.

Is this what closeness is all about? Is this how family ties are formed?

Once they were outside the shopping complex, Romita drew in a deep breath. She felt better – away from the closed heat of the market. But the air was still and hot even outside. Shops downed shutters and business rolled up for the day. Outside the south gate, a group of young boys were standing, blowing soap bubbles into the air. The lights reflected on the suds, throwing up a spectrum of colours in tiny droplets. Colourful globules floated around, staying suspended in mid-air for a while, and bursting as they hit the passers-by. Palash broke into a run after a taxi. Romita stared mesmerised at the floating bubbles.

"Taxee ..." he yelled. Getting a taxi in this city was almost like winning a lottery. It was worse after sundown, when the whims of the drivers decided one's fate.

Palash stuck his head gleefully through the window of a car.

"Which way?" asked the driver.

"South. Tollygunge."

"I'm going north." The driver smiled philosophically and pressed on the accelerator. Palash lost his balance and almost fell face downwards. Scrambling to his feet, he ran for the next one but he soon lost out in the battle of wits. He clenched his fists in impotent rage, muttering obscenities against the city's taxi drivers at large. His fair, girlish face would always flush at moments of such blind rage.

Romita laughed, "Come on, let's go ... let's walk up to Esplanade and take the Metro."

"We should have brought the car today," Palash said bitterly.

"That car!" Romita smirked. "You should sell off that prehistoric Morris Minor and get yourself a bicycle instead. You can at least pedal down to office every morning."

"Pulling my leg, aren't you? Can't you guess the sentimental value attached to that car? It was my grandfather's heart and soul. Almost a second wife! My uncles wanted to sell it off but Baba chose to keep the car during the division of our ancestral property. The car drinks petrol in gallons, still Baba decided to keep it." Switching over to light-hearted banter, he said mockingly, "Just you wait! I'll tell Baba that you were calling your grand mom-in-law names!"

"No, please don't."

"Baba won't say a thing to you, even if I do."

"Why won't he? Because I'm a new bride?"

"Uhuh! Because you're the pretty bride."

In a green South Indian sari with contrasting borders, Romita knew she looked good and quietly accepted the praise as her due.

The couple walked down the crowded Lindsay Street. All of a sudden a Maruti almost ran into them making Palash pull Romita back, crushing her fingers against the coral and moonstone ring she wore.

"Oof!" Romita exclaimed in pain. "You, Leos, are like peasants – boorish and rough."

Palash laughed aloud. "And you Geminis are a trifle too delicate."

"That reminds me," said Romita, inwardly ashamed that the subject had completely slipped her mind. "Sri Yogi advised you to wear a gem for good luck and health."

"Have you told Ma? She knows a good jeweller who doesn't cheat his customers."

"It had completely slipped my mind. What is your mother's zodiac sign?"

"Could be Taurus."

"I think it's Libra. Your father could well be a Taurus. Taurians are slightly conservative,"

"Why? What old-fashioned traits have you spotted in Baba?"

"Well, I heard your father complaining to your mother about the lehenga-choli that I wore to your cousin's wedding. He refused to see her point that it was the fashion, nowadays. 'A new bride of the Choudhurys of Kashunde seen at a family wedding in a backless dress?'" he kept saying.

"That's how Baba is. Hard to please – Couldn't leave his old views and values behind at Kashunde when he moved to Golf Club Avenue. Can't blame him though – he belongs to an older generation, after all."

"Tell me, was my dress too daring?"

"Daring! Yes!" Palash screwed up his eyes and made a face. "Anybody could have fallen for you."

Romita nudged Palash gently. Of late, Palash was never at a loss for words. He had been shy and quiet with her during their honeymoon in Manali. Palash would sit next to Romita, silent and still, during the long evenings they had spent together with the river Bipasha flowing swiftly past the hotel's balcony. Romita had had to break the ice and start a conversation.

She would say in a bantering tone, "Didn't you go to an English-medium co-educational school?"

"Yes, I did."

"And spent about four years in an engineering college hostel? Was it a college hostel or a monastery?"

Palash wouldn't speak but sit looking silently at Romita for a while. He would then look away, lower his eyes, touch her hands and ask, " Do you think I am a monk?"

"Why are you so silent then?"

"Beauty is to be appreciated quietly."·

"What is so beautiful? The river? The icy peaks? The pine forests perhaps? Or is it the gurgling sound of the water?"

"You."

How wonderfully soft and sweet the word sounded on Palash's lips. "Y-o-u!" ... It was not a word but the soft rustling breeze among the pine woods of Manali.

Even now, the word created waves of music in Romita's heart. She knew she was beautiful, uncommonly so. She had heard people say it a million times since her birth. She had skin as smooth and white as conch shell, lips that were as shapely as young bamboo leaves, thick dark eyelashes, a glowing face and a complexion that resembled peach-red Kashmiri apples. She knew the adjectives by heart now – a little too well, perhaps; she had heard them so often. But still, that single 'you' was enchanting ... Romita firmly believed in luck. She also believed that it was Lady Luck alone who had reserved Palash solely for her – to be her husband.

She stopped by a foodstall.

"Want bhelpuri?" she asked.

"You mean, have it here? On the road? Ugh! Enteric diseases are on the rise. Haven't you been reading the papers?"

"Let's not bother with those who are sick. Falling ill has nothing to do with whether you eat junk food off the street or not." Romita lowered her voice. "Watch that lady tucking in. She seems to be in the pink of health, in spite of eating this kind of food." Palash threw a glance at the enormous woman. Phuchkas slipped down her throat in smooth succession.

Palash whispered, "That's not good health. That's plain fat. Have you ever watched a circus hippopotamus gobble down cauliflowers? She reminds me of its huge open mouth. If you eat the way she does, I'm sure you will be just as healthy."

"Okay, okay. I don't mind being that. Now will you please order two bhelpuris? And I want them swimming in sauce."

Romita ate her bhelpuri noisily, feeling happy.

"Suppose Baba saw the new bride standing on the road, gobbling ..." Palash exclaimed in mock fear.

"Nothing would happen. Baba would stop and simply order one for himself. Baba loves food, I know that."

"He hardly eats these days. The doctor has struck off most goodies from his diet. No salt. No sweets." Palash frowned. "I keep worrying about Baba, you know. He has suffered one stroke already, gone through a lot of stress while settling the annual accounts at the end of the year. Business is a permanent source of tension. At present, there's the pressing issue of a fresh O. D. that needs to be looked into."

Palash's family ran an old business making scientific equipments for schools and colleges. But of late the demand had plummeted. Palash's father planned to update his portion of the factory. However, that was not so simple. Bank loans were not easy to come by. Stock market scams, with unscrupulous key players like Harshad Mehta* juggling with the share rates, had shaken the very foundation of the country's banking system.

"Can't we admit Baba to a nursing home for a few days and have him go through a thorough check-up?" Romita said helpfully.

"Yes. Even Dada thinks that would be best thing to do. I should get Baba examined by a good cardiologist. In fact, we have an appointment with Dr. Sumit Keshan, at seven in the evening this Friday."

"How strange! You've fixed the appointment for Friday! Aren't you supposed to visit my parents with me on that day?"

"Oh no!" Palash shut his eyes and shook his head. "It simply slipped my mind. Can't I visit your parents the next day? I can even stay overnight."

Romita turned her face away. She had told Palash about the evening's engagement well in advance, even reminded him of it later. How could he possibly forget all about it?

Her aunt from Jabalpur would be visiting her parents that

---

*Harshad Mehta, a stock-broker was involved in a financial scam along with some public sector banks.

evening. Her aunt hadn't been able to attend Romita's wedding and that was the why her parents had insisted that both come over for dinner. It was a very special occasion.

Palash simply had no business taking his father's entire responsibility on his shoulders, Romita thought indignantly. Palash's brother did nothing apart from lazing in his father's factory, from ten in the morning to five in the evening. And her sister-in-law never lifted a finger to help with the housework. So, why couldn't they take their father to the doctor? Romita had planned to spend the Friday chatting with her cousin Mahasweta. She longed to meet her and revive the old times – they would be meeting after years! One and a half, or was it two? Romita yearned for a good gossip. She had so many things to tell her after her marriage. It would be awkward if she visited her parents' home in Barasat, without Palash! What an absolute mess this was, with her personal likes and dislikes entangled with the wishes and whims of this young man, who was still a fairly new acquaintance. And worse – even his family played a major role here!

Romita sighed in exasperation. Was this what family bonding was all about?

Palash muttered to himself. "Baba needs a change, he would feel refreshed if he spent a few days with his Gurudev at the ashram perhaps ...?"

Romita listened with an expressionless face.

~

At the Esplanade Metro station, clusters of people stood watching a video recording of the World Cup cricket match between India and South Africa. Palash had also stopped a few seconds to watch the match. Romita pulled at his arm.

"No you shan't. You mustn't look elsewhere while I'm with you. It has to be just me, and nobody else."

The office crowd had thinned out. But random pockets of people stood in queues, waiting for their train to arrive.

Romita managed to get a seat for herself in the train. An elderly man, about to sit down, courteously offered her the seat. Romita wasn't a wee bit surprised at the man's polite gesture. The world treated beautiful women with a certain amount of awe; such favours came their way easily enough. She firmly believed that it was her due.

Palash holding on to the overhead rod bent towards her.

"Your sister didn't write back, did she?" he asked.

"She will. People are extremely busy out there. It's not like working in government jobs here."

"You're right. Abroad, everybody has to work hard for a living," Palash was quick to respond. "Let's move to Canada and settle there. Why not ask your brother-in-law to send me a job voucher?"

Romita's secret wound bled afresh. Didi wasn't half as beautiful as she was. Yet, she had managed to get herself a NRI husband. However rich and noble Palash's family lineage might be, there was a lack somewhere. Would Palash succeed in climbing the ladder of success as fast as Mihir, her sister's husband, had done? There were few future career prospects for government engineers in this country.

Mihir's company had a network across three continents; he had to travel so much he couldn't spend more than eight months a year in Canada. But he was also an engineer like Palash. Somehow, sheer beauty had not won Romita the top place in the marriage market. She was a loser in spite of her beauty.

"If you want, you should try yourself. Why should we ask others to help?" Romita said, a little short.

Palash was taken aback at the sudden harshness in her tone. The train roared down the shadowy length of the tunnel, dappled in light and shade. The mechanical voice announced each station... Park Street, Maidan, Rabindra Sadan... the compartments had become a little more crowded after Bhowanipore. Palash sat down next to Romita when a seat fell vacant, and asked, "Why are you so quiet? Are you angry?" Romita smiled at the half-embarrassed expression on Palash's face.

"Remember, it has to be Saturday and not Friday."

"What are you talking about? What Friday?"

"It has to be my house on Friday. Keep Saturday for your father's appointment with the doctor," said Romita, adding with a twinkle in her eye, "Things will take a rather unpleasant turn otherwise." The train had surfaced from the underground. Romita could hear the lashing of a violent storm outside. The sullen sky at Esplanade had turned into a romping nor'wester in Tollygunge. The crazy rain, smudged the physical outlines and blurred everything into one mass of grey dullness.

The platform was crowded. People rushed in, trying not to get wet, choosing a suitable spot to wait, from where they would hop into a bus or a rickshaw as soon as it stopped raining. Palash jostled through the crowd with Romita and waited inside the porch. Five or six motorcycles were getting drenched in the incessant downpour. The roadlamps glowed dully behind the sheet of water. Palash said good humouredly, "Just look at those two-wheelers. Getting drenched like a herd of buffaloes. See why I don't want to buy one of those? I would buy a four-wheeler instead."

Romita frowned, her eyebrows moved like lightning across the sky.

"I've heard that line too often. In fact, you've been planning to buy one for the past couple of months," she said.

"I beg your pardon. I've already spoken to CITI bank about this project. Thirty percent down payment. The rest can be paid in monthly instalments over five years."

A sudden blast of rain drenched Romita completely. She didn't have time to cover herself. At the same moment an unfamiliar touch on the exposed small of her back made Romita jump. She turned around and found herself face to face with the owner of the hand. It was a handsome, strapping young man of about twenty-one, in a colourful baggy shirt, with a thin gold chain around his neck. He didn't look normal, had a vulgar, disgusting gaze. Romita moved closer to Palash. She pulled her sari tightly across the exposed portions of her body and covered her back. Waist. Navel. Another dirty hand touched her body. Romita moved even closer to Palash. Her instincts told her that the boy was not alone. There were others. In front. Behind her. Next to her. Someone pinched her buttocks hard. Aghast, Romita instinctively shrunk . A muscular, well-built, bearded man gave Palash a gentle push without any apparent reason. Amazed, Palash looked back. The man retorted crudely, "Stand straight, can't you?"

"What did I do? It was you who pushed me."

"Shut up! Don't give me all that rot!" the man said, resorting to the contemptuous "tui" instead of "aapni." He pushed again, this time harder .

Someone, in a blue corduroy jacket, called out, "Hey you b***, stand straight."

"Why do you have to be so rude? *You* kept pushing and falling on me!"

"Shut your trap! Who fell on you, you f***?"

"You bloody scoundrel!"

"How dare you abuse, you s** of a b***!" In a flash Baggy shirt pulled Romita away from Palash . "Showing off your manhood to this slut, huh?"

Palash was speechless with anger. Romita pulled at his hand.

"Come away. Just a pack of ruffians!"

One of them gave a lewd laugh. It was clear that the young men had planned to stage a mishap.

A man in a black T-Shirt held Romita's chin,"What a sweet voice you have!" he smiled

Palash lost his senses. He pounced on the man and clutched hold of his collar.

"Just see what they are doing," he cried, addressing the crowd gathered around them. "They have pushed me and now are trying to misbehave with my wife."

"Shut up. I'll give you a tight slap – Strip off your pants."

The crowd stood silent.

Palash screamed in maddening rage. " Who'll slap me? Which saala f***** has the courage?"

The burly, bearded man gave Palash a push and he fell face flat on the ground. Baggy shirt and black T-shirt held Romita's hands in an iron grip from both sides. The crowd stood motionless, as if watching the shooting of a film sequence. Palash got back to his feet and charged at the men like an angry bull. The burly man intercepted him midway. Meanwhile, in the scuffle that followed the crowd ran helter skelter in fright.

Romita screamed, "What do you think you're doing? Let me go, let me go, I say."

"*Aaj na chhorunga tujhhe dum duma dum*," Baggy-shirt lisped out a popular film number.

Swaying with the song's rhythm, Black T-shirt bumped his hip against Romita's. There wasn't a speck of anger on their faces.

Imitating the gestures and dance movements of film actors, all of them joined in chorus - "*Dil mein hai toofan bada, dum duma dum; Naach meri jaan zara, dum duma dum.*"

Palash put in all effort to release himself from the grip of the bearded man...

"You dirty b******s," he screamed. "I'll kick your..."

The man slapped him hard across his face, "Keep quiet, you s**of a b****."

Romita desperately looked for help around her, "For god's sake, do something …. Please help us."

A soft murmur rose within the crowd. Snatches of conversation, bits of remarks, sparked off like fireworks only to burn out in a moment.

"Let her go, dada. Come to your senses."

"One shouldn't lose one's temper when out with a woman."

"But he was provoked."

"Why don't you fight it out between the two of you. Why involve the woman at all?"

"What these chaps need is a good thrashing. You get me? All their fingers and toes should be beaten out of shape."

The middle-aged man stopped in the middle of his sentence, doubling up with pain, as blue jacket kicked him. The murmur died within minutes. The crowd fell silent once again. Silence lay heavy, broken only by the sound of howling wind and lashing rain. In this impotent jungle of humanity, their paths now clear of obstacles, the brave heroes decided to have some fun with Romita. Her sari was pulled down to bare her breasts while black T-shirt held her tightly in his arms, singing lustily, *"Choli ke peechey kya hai.."*

A strange, helpless anguish coupled with an overwhelming sense of humiliation seized Romita. She lost control over the situation, unable to fully understand what was happening around her. The bearded man had cornered Palash, and pinned him to a wall. Palash lost all strength to resist.

Jhinuk had been standing at a distance, lost in the crowd. She hadn't left the platform as it had been raining. When the rain seemed to lessen, she pushed her way through the crowd and stopped dead watching the heroes at work. She couldn't believe her eyes. Was it real? Or a fantasy? Suddenly, something snapped inside her head. Clutching her bag tightly with her hands, she charged into the crowd.

"You brutes!" she screamed, "Leave her alone, will you? Let her go. You look decent enough.."

As the man in the blue jacket moved towards her, she clutched her heavy bag and swung it in the air, blindly swishing it in all directions. Romita managed to free herself from black T-shirt's grip. Gathering her sari, and draping it around herself, she saw black T-shirt inching towards her saviour.

Jhinuk screamed contemptuously at the crowd, "What are you gaping at? So many of you have been watching this silently? A young woman being molested right in front of your eyes?"

Black T-shirt twisted Jhinuk's wrist. He slapped her hard on the jaw and almost threw her towards the motorbikes. Jhinuk promptly got up and charged back, wiping the blood from her lips. By this time, Baggy shirt and Black T-shirt had dragged Romita out in the rain. Baggy shirt started up his motorcycle while Black T-shirt pushed Romita towards the vehicle, trying to force her down between Baggy shirt and himself.

The bearded man left Palash alone, and ran to start up another motorcycle, the man in the jacket ran for the third. Jhinuk scrambled across to Romita and pulled her with all her might. In the tussle that followed, they both went rolling down in the slush.

The crowd came to its senses at last. Perhaps after watching

Jhinuk! A couple of men charged towards Baggy shirt and Black T-shirt. A few ran along with Palash towards the waiting motorcycles. Within seconds, they sped away with a thunderous roar. Blue jeans kicked his vehicle to start it up, but the dripping wet two-wheeler kept stubbornly silent. He kicked it once again. And again. His burly mate came back to help his friend. He drove his vehicle into the crowd, making people scatter.

"Come on Suman," he yelled, "Leave that bloody junk."

Blue jacket shoved and elbowed his way recklessly out, through the crowd into safety. The other man clambered on to the waiting motorcycle which zipped through the night air, vanishing in a few seconds.

Romita sat in the slush, shivering. Palash pulled her up to her feet. Panting, he blurted out in disgust, "It's a dustbin. The city's a filthy dustbin." Jhinuk's dupatta lay in the slush. She picked it up and pressed it against her bleeding lower lip. Her bag lay torn at her feet. Only the bubblegum remained intact in her mouth. She chewed it restlessly, glaring at the crowd. "A city is never filthy. It's the people who live there. A whole batch of eunuchs simply stood and watched the drama. The shame of it all!"

Romita left Palash and caught hold of Jhinuk's hands. The crowd had by now closed in around the three. Words couldn't be distinguished from the thousand murmurs that rose. Jhinuk eyed the faceless crowd with contempt.

"You had enough fun watching this drama," she said. "Can I now expect you to accompany us to the police station at least?" She turned to Palash. "We should file an FIR immediately. We must go to the police after it stops raining."

Palash silently nodded in agreement, almost like a robot. Romita's frozen emotions and rising pain struggled to gush out in a flood of tears. She was hit by a sudden nausea. Gritting her teeth to control herself, Romita clung to Jhinuk, and burst into tears.

Nor'westers come and go in no time. By the time the three climbed down to the pavement, it had stopped raining.

"Wait," said Jhinuk. "Let me note down the number of this motorcycle." She walked up to the abandoned vehicle with Palash. Romita draped her sari tightly around herself trying to cover her torn blouse. She looked in vain for the crowd which had gathered. Everybody was rushing home.

Not a soul came along with them.

Chapter Three

"Auntie, flowers ... Ma has sent them for you."

A tiny girl with a cherubic face stood with a bunch of roses in her small hands. Like many butterflies, the children surrounded Jhinuk.

"Auntie, did you hit the goondas hard"?

"Auntie do you know karate? Kung-fu"?

"Didn't you have a gun with you? An AK 47?"

"You must pump bullets into the villains and kill them. Rat-tat-tat-t-t-t-t!"

"Don't worry, auntie. When I grow up, I'm going to make mince meat out of all bad men."

Jhinuk was so touched that tears came into her eyes.

"Thank you, thank you children," she managed to mutter. "Go and sit down please."

Fresh morning sunlight streamed in through the window, flooding the room with glowing warmth. Jhinuk felt her emotions rising once again. She had felt the heat come and go over the past two days. An evening's bravado; a few excited moments at the police station– the next day all the papers carried a small news item: "Srobona Sarkar, a young school teacher from Vikramshila Mahavihar, endangers herself to uphold modesty of Romita Chowdhury, a housewife."

Their house was flooded with reporters that same afternoon.

Yesterday's papers had been full of spine-chilling descriptions of the incident; the editorial had gone overboard with praise; she was flooded with greetings from neighbours, friends and relatives. The speedy string of events had made Jhinuk gloat in a surge of self-satisfaction. 'Srobona Sarkar' had become renowned overnight. She had become a star, had set an example. Where would she store all her newfound joy?

Not for a moment had she anticipated this turn of events. The day had been like any other – tuned to a steady chord. School in the morning. Back from work. A short nap in the afternoon, followed by small jobs and errands. Meeting friends in the evening. A moment's grief and then a fleeting joy. Everything was perfectly cut to size, to fit into its respective slot. A sudden nor'wester had turned the slots topsy-turvy.

The papers were full of such reports, these days. Housewife murdered — gang raped. Atrocities against women. Outrage of modesty. But all that was just news. People gulped it down over their morning cups of tea, had discussions and heated arguments on the train, the bus, in office, at home, basking in the heat of the excitement and forgetting about it all in due course. Could anybody ever imagine that such news would be part of one's life? Did Jhinuk ever anticipate that she would be a witness to this grisly incident – that she would be right there when it happened? That a moment's spark of excitement would throw her into a whirlpool of events? She was not a mere witness but the key figure – the heroine, playing the main part! Jhinuk had at last struck success, she had made a name for herself!

Jhinuk sat in the staff room, sniffing at the roses, during break. Their fragrance lost, they were all dry now, but they were still bright and colourful.

"Your lips are still swollen Srobona," Dipika said. "Have you got hurt elsewhere?" she asked. Madhuri was Jhinuk's best friend in the school, though she was a little older. Before Jhinuk could answer, she chipped in "Oh, you didn't see what she looked like yesterday, or the day before – with swollen and puffed out cheeks, she was a perfect sight! Is your fist any better Jhinuk? Got an X-ray done?"

It was a small staff room – a few chairs, two steel cupboards and a wooden bookrack were placed around a large table in the centre. A huge ceiling fan droned above. Jhinuk walked up from her corner seat to a chair placed right under it and sat down. "I was badly hurt," she said. "Should have taken two more days off. My parents didn't want me to get back to work so soon. But I had to come because the school is closing down for the summer vacation."

Roma was chalking out a holiday lesson plan for the kids. She, like Gitali, had taught Jhinuk in the primary classes. With a voice oozing sympathy, she said, "It was a miracle. God saved you. Fighting so many of those ruffians alone isn't funny, you know!"

Gitali asked, "What did they look like? Hefty and rough, were they? Were they armed?"

"I didn't notice. But I *did* notice that they were drunk, with their eyes half-closed. Leering monsters! They didn't look like professional gangsters though." Jhinuk leaned back. "There's a new class in society now — the cash-rich– they move around in expensive clothes, throw their money about, and are fluent in English. They have a good time with their new Maruti cars and motorbikes – you'll spot quite a number of such young men on the city streets."

Mita chipped in, snapping her lunch box open. "You mean they belong to wealthy homes?" she asked.

"Not really," Gitali made a face. "Their cash comes from bribes, through the back door, or from the share market."

Roma put the exercise books aside, "How was the woman dressed? Decent enough, or was it very provocative?"

"Sari and blouse," replied Jhinuk with a shrug. "Well ... the neckline was pretty low, I admit. But I didn't find it immodest."

"Oh, so that was the reason. You never told the media about this bit," Lekha popped a slice of apple into her mouth. "A wet, rainy evening. That raving beauty with a low neckline! Enough to turn on a saint!"

"That's not right, Lekhadi," Dipika immediately protested. " In that case women in bikinis on the beaches would have men running after them all the time. Where's the need for education and civility? We should be living in jungles."

"Speaking of men's civility and education, the less said the better," Lekha chipped in, raising her voice. She was still smarting from the memory of her year-old divorce. Her forty-six-year-old husband flirted with several women even after fourteen years of marriage. This led to big, screaming fights and beatings, which finally ended in a divorce.

Lekha lived alone with her two young daughters. Now, she declared in a firm voice, "Men are naturally greedy. It's only girls like Srobona who can put them in place." Mita was a die-hard man-hater. Dark, and quite plain, she had suffered enough embarrassment and humiliation at the hands of the families of prospective grooms who had rejected her. She was no longer young, and stood almost no chance of tying the knot now. "Men are like dogs," she hissed, "the only difference being that the former are almost always in heat."

Everybody was about to burst into laughter when Geetali chided them softly, "Haven't I told you several times that you are not to use foul language in the staffroom? Don't forget the fact that all of you are teachers here."

Dipika quickly changed the topic. "Hey Srobona," she asked. "Have these fellows been arrested?"

"It would have been in the papers if they were," observed Madhuri.

"Oh, forget the newspapers! They just print juicy titbits to increase their sale. Haven't you noticed how they focus on a news item, spin tales for a couple of days, then suddenly forget about it?"

"There's a positive side to the newspaper running the story. The police have no option but to arrest the scoundrels. They won't be able to hush up the case even if they want to. Isn't that right, Srobona?"

"Yes. And that's going to add to my work," shrugged Jhinuk. "I shall probably have to go to the police station and identify them."

"Won't you feel nervous facing those ruffians all over again?" Roma asked, perturbed.

Jhinuk waved her off. "No auntie," she said. "They won't dare harm me. If they're arrested, the police will make mincemeat of them."

"Let's wait and see when the police arrest them," said Madhuri. "You were lucky you could, at least, file an FIR that night."

"It's not that bad, Madhuridi. The O.C. was not an unpleasant guy. He was polite enough to ask me to sit down when we entered his room and listened carefully to every little detail of the incident. "Don't you worry,' he said. 'If the motorcycle is still there then those chaps are in for it. I'll send someone right away to collect the bike and bring it to the police station.' I have a friend, Sulagna, whose uncle is with the Lalbazar police station. She told me that the news had set Lalbazar HQ on fire. The police commissioner has personally called up the police station to make enquiries!"

"That's all they are capable of – making enquiries! Two days have passed, but where are the culprits? No sign of them!"

"I suspect the duty officer's up to some mischief. He kept asking me awkward questions."

Ranjana's wedding had been fixed for July. Sitting away from the rest of her colleagues, she was listening to the discussion. Suddenly curious, she asked, "Like what? What kind of questions?"

Jhinuk threw a glance at Gitali, then lowered her voice, "Did they actually outrage her modesty? Or was it just an attempt? Were there any bruises anywhere?" She lowered her voice even more, "Where exactly did they touch? Which part of the body? A medical test should be done immediately if a particularly vulnerable part of the body has been injured."

"The police are generally uncivilized, they can rape you simply with their words alone. They turn chicken when it comes to work. Be it ruffians or the police, they are all males, after all." Jhinuk didn't like Mita's comments. True, the questions hadn't been too polite, but did anyone have an option? The police had to ask a few routine questions. However, she couldn't ignore what Mita said. How could the police allow those men to move around freely after going through the minutest details of the case?

Gitali was cleaning her lunch box at the wash-basin. "It's hard to believe that this is the same Srobona we knew – a girl who sat in class with a frightened look on her face, who would burst into tears if you happened to look at her sternly. I remember her once being upto some mischief and Pranatidi locking her inside the durwan's room. What a state I found her in when I opened the door! Bloodshot eyes, hiccupping every minute. That same girl is now beating up goondas, marching up to the police station, answering back to the reporters."

"True," said Roma, coming up to Jhinuk and touching her chin lovingly with her fingers. "The very mention of the police station makes me feel weak in the knees."

Jhinuk's ego puffed up. A single nor'wester had boosted her confidence a hundred times. Walking tall, in speech and gait, she resembled the queen swan.

There was always a small get-together of teachers in Sunita's room before the school broke up for holidays. The primary section met separately, earlier in the morning, while the high school party was held later in the afternoon. It was supposed to create a special bonding between the school and the teachers. The staff however, had nicknamed it the "laddoo party," nothing but laddoos and chanachur were served ever since the school was established.

This year too, there was no exception. The only addition was Sunita's speech in Jhinuk's honour.

"Srobona is not only a member of our staff but also a former student of this school," she declared eloquently. "That she had been inspired by the principles and guidelines set by our school and has shown such exemplary courage, brings honour to the school and makes us proud." She rambled on, "Mr. Sengupta has suggested that the school felicitate Srobona at a special function when it re-opens after summer. Both morning and day sections are to be present at this function. Mr. Sengupta favoured that arrangement."

Normally, Sunita's eloquence would have made Jhinuk smile quietly to herself. Today, she was blushing with pride. She whispered, "Madhuridi, just look how Auntie carries on!" Madhuri pinched Jhinuk good-humouredly. "You can keep the certificate of honour," she said. "Just hand over any gifts you get to me, provided you get something more than laddoos."

Jhinuk floated out of school. A few tired kids waited at the gate to be taken home. Jhinuk knew very well how mischievous a couple of them were. These kids weren't afraid of anything in life. The old durwan, Jeevanda was the only person they respected and feared. It was probably because of his khaki uniform.

"Look at the time!" exclaimed Madhuri. "It's 12.40 p.m. and there's no sign of the mothers!"

"There's peace at home as long as the kids aren't around. I wonder what they'll turn out to be!"

"Become like your goondas, you mean?"

"Possibly! As children, those men must have been to a school like ours – these kids already sing the songs those guys were singing. They seem to be born with guns and pistols in their blood!" Jhinuk was lost in her thoughts. "What an unnerving idea, Madhuridi," she said at last. "I wonder how our children are going to turn out."

"Counting chickens before they are hatched! Get married first. How's your man, Tunir? Any news of him? Is he jumping with joy, singing paeans to your might?"

"Almost." Jhinuk smiled. "He rushed to our house the very next morning, after reading the papers."

Jhinuk stumbled in her eloquence. She had expected Tunir last evening, after the papers had run her story. But Tunir hadn't come;

neither had he called! Was he too busy with work? Caught up with some important office project?

Madhuri hadn't stopped grinning even on the tram home.

"You were simply born lucky! Adding new feathers to your cap – that's how your life is! You can hand over to me a few that slip off."

"What will you do with them?"

"Well, I'll show them off to my mom-in-law. She might be pleased to see bright, colourful feathers and her heart might soften a little – have some mercy on me."

"Rubbish! You love sucking up to your mother-in-law all the time. Stop whining now!"

"Do I have a choice? She's eccentric and she's old," Madhuri's voice trailed off. "It all began after my father-in-law died. She became fastidious about keeping body and soul clean and pure. Doesn't allow her five-year-old grandson into her room if he's not in fresh clean clothes. Little wonder that she won't allow cooks and domestic helps to step into her kitchen or her household."

"It's all Tridibda's fault; he's quite spineless. Can't he explain his wife's problems to his mother – make her realise that you have a job – and all that back-breaking housework is an additional load?"

"Tell me, which man would choose to interfere in household affairs?"

"Still – it's wrong of Tridibada. A pile of household chores waiting to be finished as soon as you get back home from work everyday – why, that's torture! Taking orders from the old lady – washing clothes, cleaning dishes, cooking dinner – Tridibda should at least help you with the housework. Or is that below his dignity?"

"It's fate," Madhuri smiled weakly. "Your fate is all pretty feathers and Tunir. Mine – that old woman and that husband! Nothing exciting happens in my life, like it has done for you. At least I could have shown off my prowess and flexed my muscles at home for my husband to see. I would have gained some weight."

Madhuri was plump enough. She would often rush to her doctor, get herself an elaborate diet chart – which she would forget in the next seven days – and eat all the wrong food.

Jhinuk eyed Madhuri. "Good heavens!" she exclaimed. "You want to gain more weight?"

Madhuri burst out into a peal of laughter which cut through the air. The afternoon tram was almost empty, and people turned around to look. Madhuri consciously lowered her voice. "Once you settle down to holy wedlock, and you produce a couple of kids, I'll keep a watch on your weight too. Coming for an evening show with me?"

Madhuri could switch over to new topics with an uncanny ease. How she had the energy and the enthusiasm to rush off to movies, shops and fairs, after all the endless chores of the day, was beyond comprehension. Perhaps this was Madhuri's quiet revolt – against the daily pile of work that left her gasping for breath – against the exploitation. Her will to live and breathe was as strong as that of the desert cactus.

"Not today," Jhinuk replied. "Tunir might drop in, this

evening." Madhuri got off the tram before it reached its depot at Tollygunge. Jhinuk generally took a rickshaw home from the tram depot, or she walked. Six years ago, when her family bought the new flat and moved into it, the neighbourhood was still green with trees and had several natural lakes and ponds. Over the years, the city had extended its octopus arms into the last green patches and had gradually sucked them up.

Jhinuk crossed the road and stopped. The Metro station porch lay silent and sleepy in the scorching afternoon sun. A few street dogs wandered about, looking for shade. There was none.

The empty porch looked so self-contained! Almost indifferent to its surroundings.

Chapter Four

*J*hinuk entered their apartment and came to a dead stop. Thamma! Sujata had curtained off the sitting lounge from the dining space – the pretty cream net curtains were pulled to one side of the sleek curtain rod. Mrinalini sat at one end of the dining table.

"Thamma!" Jhinuk bounced across to her in an overwhelming surge of joy and hugged her grandmother tightly. She took deep breaths. That same old faint, but sweet smell! Mrinalini's cool body would always give off that particular scent. It was only Jhinuk who got the scent, nobody else did. Perhaps it was an odour born out of seething agony and deep longing – the agony of a lonely life in an old age home and a longing for those close to her heart – an odour much like the musk of a musk-deer.

Mrinalini was quietly enjoying her granddaughter's caresses.

Jhinuk finally flopped into a chair next to her and asked, "Why are you out in the hot sun?"

"Your summer holidays have begun also – why were you out?"

"I went to renew my Employment Exchange card. Think of your age and mine!" Jhinuk rubbed her cheek against Mrinalini's, inhaling the scent once again. "I would have visited you in a couple of days," she said.

"She didn't have a choice. She had to come." Sujata's spoke with a quiet pride. "With her granddaughter creating such turmoil, she had to. Everybody is worried."

Smiling pleasantly Mrinalini said, "I've chosen to live away from my family – have taken vanaprastha* that's all. That doesn't imply I have retired from life, does it? I haven't been able to free myself from earthly ties, from the worries and tensions of family life. I tried calling you on the telephone several times from a shop opposite our Home – couldn't get a connection between Behala and Tollygunge in four days! But my dear, you look well enough. I don't think you were seriously hurt! Those newsmen must have blown the story out of proportion and added a little colour. I was quite nervous after reading the news report."

"Wasn't she hurt! You wouldn't have said that if had you seen this daredevil girl of mine that same night. Right cheek swollen and puffed out, blood smeared all over, the girl couldn't move her hand! Her dupatta was torn to pieces, mud splashed all over her body, and her hair ... a perfect mess ..."

---

*Vanaprastha is the last stage in a Hindu's life when he renounces everything to go and live in the forests.

"Ah Ma, will you stop that? No Thamma, I'm fine now, fit as a fiddle – as fresh as flowers ready for sale in a shop. Sparkling fresh!"

"Rubbish! Even last night, you were groaning in pain. You could sleep only after you took a painkiller."

Mrinalini held Jhinuk's hands for a closer look. "Hum, you left wrist is still quite swollen," she observed.

Jhinuk smiled shamefacedly, "They twisted my left wrist hard. I simply couldn't move it that night. Baba gave me a hot compress."

Sujata was closing all the windows. She did it every afternoon to keep the house cool. Even then, the heat was overwhelming – it seemed to seep in through the walls, drip down the ceiling. Being a top-floor flat, the heat hung in the air for a long time, even after sundown.

Mrinalini said, "Oh, your father must have had a nerve-wracking experience!"

Sujata stopped on her way to the kitchen and turned round, "Much more than that, thanks to your granddaughter. She caused us so much worry. I waited out in the balcony – it was so late – past nine, finally it got past ten! Your son was so agitated that he couldn't sit still. He kept going down to the ground floor and climbing back to the fourth. Later, he hunted out her friends' telephone numbers and called them up – he was so terribly nervous and tense. She's a girl after all ... her friend informed us that she had left for home hours back – around half past eight ... and that girl doesn't show up before eleven... your son was simply ... well,

I won't be able to describe ... the condition he was in!"

"Oh, come on tell me. He was all jittery and shaking with fright, wasn't he? Mrinalini remarked flatly, "As if I don't know my son well. Does he possess any emotions other than fear and worry?"

Sujata cast a quick, sullen look at her mother-in-law and stomped off into the kitchen.

"You're right," Jhinuk agreed. "Baba can't control himself – tends to over-react to everything. He was panic-stricken when he saw me that night. But the very next day when he saw my name in the papers he was overjoyed."

"Those aren't extremes dear, that is normal. If you limit your world to a tiny, confined space and shut your eyes to everything beyond, then you *do* react in a rather unbalanced manner – grieve more, get overjoyed at the slightest instant, panic more too!"

Waves of joy were still rippling through Jhinuk's veins. She didn't pay much heed to what Mrinalini said. Sujata called out to her from the kitchen. "Go for your bath – you can talk to Thamma to your hearts content after you've eaten." Jhinuk drummed her fingers on the table, and sang out,"First lunch, then a wash. I'm hungry,I'm hungry. Thamma, I suppose you'll have lunch with me?"

"No dear. I had my lunch before I came." Mrinalini stood up, "You two have your lunch, I'll rest for a while. I should be on my way back at three sharp."

About seven years ago, just two months after Karunaketan died, Mrinalini had stubbornly left for the old age home, ignoring all pleas by her two sons and daughters-in-law. Since then, she had not spent a single night at any of their homes. She often visited, them though– stretching her stay till evening. Sometimes, she stayed on to meet her son Manas before returning home at night, later than usual, on those days.

"You can't go out in this glaring sun. Let the light soften a little," Jhinuk said.

"I haven't a choice dear. Have to drop in at Bibhu's place as well. He visited me last week. I believe Rumki is down with periodic bouts of fever."

"How could that be? Kakamoni had called us after reading the news in the papers – didn't say a word about Rumki!" Jhinuk sounded concerned. "I've asked Kakamoni several times to admit Rumki to a special school for spastic children. She would have been happier; would have made friends; she wouldn't have been ill all the time."

Sujata was laying the table. "Bibhu has never paid any heed to our advice," she complained. "Your elder son had talked to him several times, tried to explain certain things. A proper treatment would have perhaps helped the girl to study – to learn to look after herself. He had given him an address – the place is somewhere on Ballygunge Circular Road – he never bothered to go."

"Oh, leave it! People don't take kindly to advice. Who needs them?"

"Why do you say that Ma? Didn't your elder son sell off the land in Narendrapur when you advised him to do so? Why shouldn't people listen to good, sensible advice?"

Mrinalini smiled, "Don't be angry, dear. I'll tell you something.

Nobody likes being told what to do. People generally accept advice when it fits into their plan and suits their priorities. Montu needed money when he sold off the land, and that's the reason he liked my advice. Of course, he did share the money with his siblings. Montu is careful never to leave a loophole in such matters. But I had suggested the sale long ago, for Rumki's treatment. None of you had agreed then."

"We wouldn't have been able to get a good price for it at that time. The agents had asked us to wait," Sujata's voice became thicker. "Anyway, Rumki's treatment was never held up for want of money; your elder son took a loan from the cooperative, your daughter and son-in-law sent money." Sujata volleyed back steadily, but her words lacked conviction. She could never contend with the strong personality of this seventy-two year-old woman. With almost a seer's vision, Mrinalini had rightly sensed the secret reasoning that had shaped their plans then. If the land had been sold, all their shares would have had to be offered to Bibhas – for the sake of social courtesy, if not for anything else.

Mrinalini spoke out at last, perhaps in consolation, "You are all here, near me. That in itself is a relief! And you take care of all the loose ends. As for Bibhu, he has planned to waste his life; he never puts his mind to earning a steady income, doesn't care a fig about his family and household."

Jhinuk silently listened to the conversation between her mother and her grandmother. Kakamoni was extremely odd! He had married without a job or an income, and never attended office regularly when he did get one. He now spent all his time shadowing political bigwigs, running errands for them. He would catch hold of simple people, assure them of a licence and dupe them. If Baba expressed his irritation and chided him, he would wave it off and say, "Oh, you'll never understand these deals. This is called political agency. If I strike gold, I'll make a fat amount." Kakamoni would surely get a public lynching one day. And here was poor Kakima floundering – struggling to make ends meet, working away at her sewing machine at home.

The air in the room turned heavy. Sujata spoke with pity, "I feel terrible for poor Rumki – she is growing up, she looks older than her twelve years. I'll see if I can visit them in a couple of days. Let me sort out your plucky granddaughter's problems first."

Mrinalini turned back from the door leading to Jhinuk-Chhoton's bedroom. "Why do you repeatedly call her brave and plucky, dear? What daring thing has she done?"

Jhinuk stopped abruptly in the middle of her last helping of rice and curry. Sujata looked amazed, almost shocked, her eyes round with bewilderment. "Wasn't it smart and plucky of her to fight a group of gangsters, single-handed? She even walked over to the police station and fixed them. The papers had good enough reason to publish her picture."

For a moment, Mrinalini's rheumy eyes breathed fire behind her misty glasses. "Standing there, that very moment, what else could Jhinuk have done? She did exactly what any normal person would do," she said.

Jhinuk's pride was hurt, her ears turned red and she blushed deeply with resentment, as if the happy trickle of her blood cells had suddenly faced an obstruction and had stopped. Hesitating, she spoke out at last, "It's not a great feat, I know that – but don't you need guts? You have to admit that. There was a huge crowd around us. Nobody else volunteered to help!"

"What does that prove, my dear child? It's normal to watch lawlessness quietly? It's normal to be spineless? Or, that it is normal to commit a crime?"

Mrinalini went inside. Sujata finished her meal and stood up. She glanced obliquely at Jhinuk's bedroom, lowered her voice and said, "Your Thamma is weird! I've never seen her expressing joy over anything in life. Your father once went up to tell her that he had been promoted to the post of a Reader. Her response was full of innuendoes. 'The sale of your booklets with model questions and special notes will also rise. Won't it Montu?'" Jhinuk's ears had shut out all sound. She didn't hear her mother's words. The last mouthful of rice didn't move down her throat. The few days-old gurgling spring of joy had suddenly frozen to a glacier.

After a bath, Jhinuk went into her room and found Mrinalini lying on Chhoton's bed, and Sujata reading out her sister-in-law's letter to her mother-in-law. As she finished, Mrinalini said, "Have you heard Jhinuk? Ranu might come to Calcutta during Puja!" Jhinuk didn't show much interest. The long soak under a cool shower of water hadn't lessened even a fraction of her frustration. Mrinalini's words still stung her sharply. Picking up the hairbrush from the dressing table next to the bed, she said, "Pishimoni always writes she's coming. But she never does."

"She will this time. Babli's marriage is being fixed with that boy your Kakima told us about."

"Oh! What does he do?"

"Works at the electricity board." Sujata then added, "He happens to be your Kakima's cousin's son. A good enough match! We could get *you* married off as well. Babua will be around. Chhoton can also join in and help."

The flames of humiliation burned red hot in her heart but Jhinuk could still enjoy the conversation. Ma admitting that Babua would be of help to her since he was studying in Calcutta! How preferences changed according to a person's needs. Ma had once refused to let Babua stay in this house. She had made plenty of excuses: "My flat is tiny," Sujata had cribbed. "Even Chhoton doesn't feel comfortable studying here while on holiday. Would Babua be able to adjust to the lack of space and privacy? And, as you see, I'm so unwell. Can't move around because of a terrible backache. Jhinuk is on her own trip. Babua is part of the family and I would have loved to have him if things had been smooth!" How effortlessly she had shirked responsibility and had got past her aunt's request. Sujata had not cared a fig for Baba's pleas too and had remained indifferent to the subsequent tension. Poor Babua had to move from his parents' home in Alipurduar to the Jadavpur University hostel, in spite of the fact that his uncle lived in the same city – in the house that was Babua's mamarbari. Didn't Jhinuk know why Ma refused to let Babua stay with them? It was plain jealousy! With her own son spending all his academic years away in the hostel, she couldn't bear the thought of her sister-in-law's son enjoying home comforts.

Mrinalini called Jhinuk to herself, "Hey girl, come and sit beside me." Jhinuk came up to Mrinalini with a deadpan face and sat down. Mrinalini lightly caressed Jhinuk's left wrist. The touch of her blue-veined hand felt cool; it spread across her body – finally reaching the core of her being. Was this where her heart lay? Jhinuk was filled with a quiet, pleasant feeling. It was like sitting under the dark, cool shade of the towering peepul tree in the seething heat of mid-afternoon. "You had promised to bring your Tunir to me one day."

Jhinuk's frustrations had gradually subsided. "I shall," she said. "He is too busy with his office now." Sujata had got up to open a single pane of the east window. The window looked out to a few trees and a small pond. Often a pleasant wind blew in. Sujata pulled the curtains and echoed Jhinuk's words. "It's true. There's too much pressure on him. The directors feel quite lost without Tunir; he is their blue-eyed boy. He can hardly make time to visit us, where is the time to go elsewhere?" Jhinuk was mildly amused by the argument between her mother and grandmother over Tunir. Mrinalini exerted a light pressure on Jhinuk's wrist; she screamed with pain. Laughing at her reaction, Mrinalini asked, "Does it hurt you still? But my dear, have you had any news of that girl?"

Jhinuk went stiff. She hadn't spared a single thought to Romita over the last few days. She closed her eyes, trying to recapture the first lash of the nor'wester that evening, the stormy moments that followed. She tried desperately but couldn't concentrate for long. Fleeting images of the disgraced girl and the obscene gestures of the four young men and the frigid inaction of the crowd were completely drowned by visions of her own portrait in the newspapers. Or the child with the bunch of roses. The police station! The reporters! The praise in the eyes of relatives and friends. It was strange! Romita didn't feature anywhere at all. Jhinuk muttered to herself, "No, I didn't find out. Why on earth didn't I think of calling her on the telephone and finding out how she was coping with the whole thing?"

Mrinalini let go of Jhinuk's hand. "That was very wrong of you. How could you afford to think of yourself alone? After the terrible experience the girl endured that evening! Your little wounds will soon heal; think of the humiliation that poor girl has to suffer! I wonder how she is coping with it all!" Jhinuk got up immediately. What was the girl's address? What...what was it ...? She groped for the number in her mind. Oh yes! 23B, Golf Club Avenue ... that was it! Did she have a telephone at home?

Jhinuk went quickly to the sitting room. She swept through the pages of the telephone directory. Choudhury...

Choudhury ... Choudhury ... Golf Club Avenue – here was one Choudhury – Samarendra Narayan, 23B, Golf Club Avenue. Was that the girl's father-in-law's name? Perhaps it was. Jhinuk pressed the dial buttons and held the receiver to her ear. The phone was ringing. After a considerable span of time a woman's voice answered, "Hallo!"

"Does Romita Choudhury live here?"

"Yes. Who is it?"

The woman's voice slurred over her speech. She had probably

been taking a nap. Jhinuk introduced herself, "This is Srobona Sarkar. Can I speak to Romita please?"

There were a few moments of silence at the other end.

Then the voice became clear and loud, "This is Romita's mother-in-law speaking. Why do you need to speak to Romita? What is it you want?"

"Ah ... well ... I'm sorry I hadn't called earlier and enquired. How is Romita? Is she fine?"

"No, she isn't. The doctor has advised her complete rest."

"Why a doctor? What's wrong with her?"

"Well, I told you she is unwell. You can't talk to her now."

"Okay, I understand. You needn't call her. I'll visit her this evening. Can you kindly give me the directions to your house ...?"

"You needn't come," the voice was suddenly very rude, "Seeing you might increase her tension."

The telephone got disconnected with a sharp click.

Chapter
Five

*R*omita jumped out of her skin at the slight sound at the door. The magazine slipped from her hand; her heartbeat almost doubled. The slightest sound made Romita jump these days – making her teeth chatter and chill run down her spine. A strange numbness would overpower her. She often woke up, at night, frightened by the sound of her own heartbeat. Thousands of tiny spiders seem to crawl all over her body– run up and down her face, collarbones, breasts, stomach and legs. Romita would try desperately to call Palash then, wake him up from his deep slumber– but no sound would escape her voice. And sleep would elude her for the rest of the night. Even the strong sleeping pill that the doctor had prescribed didn't help. Every night was a silent, sleepless vigil.

Leena entered her room. "What's it you're reading?" she asked. Her sister-in-law's question didn't sink in. Was Leena watching her too closely these days? She seemed to notice every little physical detail, each little bodily change in her. In fact, everybody seemed to be watching her with keen interest, as if Romita had developed a sudden blemish on her body. What agony and unwarranted disruption was this, in the course of her happy, velvety smooth life?

Romita forced herself to sit up, "Is Tultul asleep?" she asked.

"I think she is, or she could be just pretending. She's particularly naughty in the afternoons."

Romita was so full of her own anxieties that she didn't much care about anybody else's woes.

Leena settled down on the bed. She looked directly at Romita's eyes. "Do you know what happened this morning?"

Romita's eyelashes quivered. "What happened?"

"How's it that you don't know? There was a call from the police station, sometime before Palash left for his office." Leena lowered her voice, "Those boys have been arrested. Someone has to go and identify them."

Such vital news but nobody had breathed a word about it to her! People in this house purposely told her nothing! Romita felt extremely indignant, humiliated. Palash generally called her aside before he left for office every morning, not to say anything but to give a smile and a routine peck on the cheek. But today he had left without saying a word. During lunch, Romita's mother-in-law had chatted endlessly about trivial things, without giving her an inkling of what was going on! Ashok – Leena's husband – often indulged in friendly banter with Romita. He cared for his brother's wife, like a young sister, joked and laughed with her, laid bare family secrets, spilling the beans. Even *he* had left with his father for the factory this morning, like any other day. Everyone in the house knew what was going on, only she was left in the dark.

Romita asked in a throbbing voice, "When were they arrested?"

"Last night."

"Would the world have turned upside down if I'd been told about it?"

Leena stretched out her legs on the bed, she tried to pacify Romita, speaking as if she was baby-talking with her two-year-old Tultul. "You know about the unwritten family code, I suppose? Every little thing is hush-hush. Your brother-in-law felt that you ought to be told about this but Palash said it might upset you further, as you were suffering from mental depression. So, Baba decided against telling you. He asked Palash to go to the police station alone, settle the matter finally and wash his hands off it."

Romita's humiliation at being practically 'cheated' by the family gradually subsided. Perhaps they were right after all. It was true, she had lost her cool completely that night, had wept uncontrollably, groaning and screaming at intervals. She had also been talking in her sleep the whole night long, "Don't you touch me! Leave me alone. Leave me, will you!"

The first few nights had been terrible. She couldn't even bear Palash's touch. Suppose *she* had to face the ruffians to identify them? Romita couldn't bear the thought of standing face to face with them, looking into their eyes. She didn't want to remember those faces even for a second, and tried hard to divert her mind to more pleasant things. In her mind, she strung together images of the happy moments she had nurtured in her heart since she was born. Baba and Ma – showering her with love. Childhood, Adolescence. Those joyful days in school and college. She remembered Baba had once bought three chocolate bars to pacify a wailing, howling little Romita, who had hurt her finger while sharpening a pencil. She cherished the memory of visiting Mother Teresa from school, loaded with gifts for the homeless orphans – clothes, bags, crayons, old toys and woollens. The Mother had come and stood before her. Romita had felt her hand lightly touching the top of her head in blessing. It was the most wonderful, heavenly experience!

But why did those four faces take clear shape and persist in her mind's eye, shattering all those impressions, erasing every other memory. Those faces haunted Romita night and day. She would shut her eyes tight and mutter the school prayer to herself for courage and peace of mind ... "When I pass through the shadowy Valley of Death, let my mind be without fear, O Lord...you are with me ... always. When I ... When I ..." she repeated. But to no effect. Terror and humiliation flooded her body and spirit – her entire being was shaken with sharp spasms of nausea – a pack of hyenas had stroked a beautiful body with their ugly, dirty paws. It was not as though men had never touched her as she grew up – the first adult kiss she had received was from a distant cousin, up in the attic of their Barasat home. And her classmate Kausik had embraced her several times in college. Men often leered at her, licking her greedily with their eyes – as if she was a juicy apple! Her feelings during those moments had been different. She had liked it when men sized her up in the mirror of their eyes. If there was greed, there was adulation too. But this was bestial! A million times uglier than the vulgar comments one had to endure in buses and trams – more pitiless than the touch of an unknown male hand in a crowded bus.

"Why do you keep on worrying night and day?" Leena asked. "It's all over. They didn't actually harm you."

"Haven't they?" muttered Romita to herself.

"No! Forget about it." Leena touched Romita on the shoulder. "Thank your lucky stars that you weren't whisked away.."

"If nothing has happened, then why does Ma keep saying that women lose their chastity forever if there's a single blemish on their bodies?"

"That's the way they talk – it's all part of an old feudal attitude."

"But Ma is quite modern in her lifestyle and her clothes!"

"I'm not exactly sure what 'modern' means in this house," Leena grimaced. "I've been married four years and have watched them pretty closely. The word 'modern' is like a dry, old coat of paint. A single tap on the plaster and the flakes crumble. Soon, you'll be made to listen to one family anecdote – of how a patriarch of the family had thrown his wife out of the house on some flimsy issue. Haven't they told you the story already?"

"No."

"They certainly will – soon enough. Our father-in-law's great grandfather or someone a few generations up the ladder, was having a good time with his chums one evening, while his son lay dying of typhoid. His wife sent him several messages. But the husband sat chatting and puffing away at his hubble-bubble, not the least worried, taking his own sweet time to go indoors. Finally, his wife came rushing into the sitting room in desperation, her head uncovered. This made her husband mad with rage. How could his wife forget her manners or lose her sense of propriety and come out in public with her head bare? Such audacity could not be tolerated. So, he immediately ordered her out of the house. And she had to leave that very moment in the clothes she stood in. Her sin? Baring her head in front of all and sundry!"

Romita tried to smile, "Come on, Baba is not like his ancestor."

"Did I say Baba was like that? Men in this family are different. And that is exactly what Ma insists we keep in mind, in order to realise how lucky we are. Our mother-in-law belongs to a curious breed. She visits beauty parlours and is up to the latest fashions but at the same time she is mighty proud of family pedigree and customs. It's all a mere show!"

Romita kept silent. Leena often indulged in criticising her mother-in-law but if Romita joined in, she would straightaway spill the beans. Initially, Romita had disliked a few of her mother-in-law's habits, particularly the way she looked down on Leena's family. She thought the family lacked class, and openly discussed their shortcomings. She often wondered what her son found so attractive in Leena and why he had fallen in love with her. During nerve-wracking fights with her mother-in-law, Leena would often unabashedly voice Romita's opinion, landing Romita in an embarrassing situation. Romita had become extremely cautious since then.

Leena was about to say something more, when a baby's cry from the adjacent room made her stand up. "There sounds Lord Krishna's flute for Radha. Let me go and pat her back to sleep." Romita stared out of the window. The summer sun glared like the bloodshot eyes of an angry criminal. The pale, colourless sky seemed to stretch to a distance. The crimson blossoms of the gulmohar tree, bending over the window, remained still. Not a single petal stirred. The earth lay silent, burning in the scorching sun.

After the sudden storm that evening, the world was back to its usual indifferent mood. The shameless afternoon continued to tick on from moment to moment. And the dispassionate world spared not a thought for the unknown fears and apprehensions that unsettled the body and mind of an obscure Romita Datta (sorry, Romita Choudhury now), of Golf Club Avenue.

~

Palash returned quite late in the evening. Romita had been waiting for him with bated breath, he didn't come upstairs, as he did on other days. He walked straight to the sitting room to meet his father instead. Romita's mother-in-law followed. Heated discussions ensued. Nobody enquired after Romita.

Romita came outside and stood in the balcony. Palash's father Samarendra had sold off his portion of the ancestral home in Howrah a few years ago and had built a new house here. The place was away from the growing jungle of houses and was comparatively less crowded. The house faced an open green, where the neighbourhood boys played cricket and football every afternoon. And as evening descended, a few lovesick couples came and settled down like pigeons in a dovecote, for a few private hours with each other.

Romita's eyes crossed the bright neon lamps down the street and floated out to the darkness beyond, where a crowd of sisu trees threw spooky shadows against the horizon. Her gaze dived into the shadows. A sudden sound behind her caught her unawares. It was Palash!

He had seated himself on a cane chair in the balcony, his face half-hidden in the light-and-shade of twilight – like the sisu trees, there were astral shadows on his face as well.

Romita's heart beat faster. She gathered courage and asked, "Did you go to the thana?"

"Who told you about the police station? Ma? Boudi?"

"How does that matter?" Romita pulled up another cane chair and sat down. "Please tell me what happened. Were they the same boys ...?"

"Hum," Palash leaned back. "Everyone of them has been arrested."

"Did they spend the night in the lock-up?"

"They were supposed to."

"Did you identify them from outside the bars?"

"Hum."

"Did you go to the thana before going to office – or after?"

"Now *you're* beginning to interrogate me like the police!" Palash sounded exasperated.

Romita fell silent. A long day at work, followed by the hassles at the police station had probably left him drained. " Men should be allowed to rest peacefully at this time of the day." That's what Ma would say when Romita as a young girl would make a beeline for her father as soon as he was back from office and complain to him about her sister. When Romita would argue indignantly. "Why shouldn't I tell Baba? Didi beats me all day, pulls my hair, hides all my toys shouldn't I tell Baba about that?"

Now, sitting between light and darkness, Romita decided that probably Ma was right. But unable to contain the anxiety brewing within her, she spoke once again, after a few minutes. "Can I ask you another question? Would you mind?"

Palash turned his face towards her.

"Did the police send for Srobonadi?"

"Since when has Srobona Sarkar become your didi?"

"Well, I don't mean it that way," Romita gulped in embarrassment. "She's older than I am, after all."

"Huh, older my foot! She's plain street smart."

"Why? What has she done?"

"Women needn't go to the police station at all for identification. But she had to go, simply to act smart, show off her worldly wisdom," Palash remarked bitterly. "A whole lot of clever talking! She's a big show-off. She kept advising me ... 'Why didn't you meet the reporters? There's no reason why anybody should feel threatened by those silly hooligans!' Huh! She even wanted to come and see you!"

"Did you ask her to come?"

"There's absolutely no need for her to come. She has got enough publicity and mileage out of it."

"You told her not to come?"

"Not directly ... said it with some tact. She should get the message clear enough."

"What did you say?"

"Well, I told her, 'You have saved my wife from dishonour. We remain ever grateful to you for that. But we don't want the women of our family to associate themselves with this vulgar incident any further.'"

Palash's voice cracked with contempt and suppressed anger, "She is a heroine for the newspapers – at the cost of your scandal."

"Scandal! What scandal?"

"If an accident – a somewhat titillating incident – is further moulded and packaged as a sensational story by the newspapers, it turns out to be the talk of the town – a scandal that the public love to lap up. Do you follow what I'm trying to say?"

The word "titillating" hit Romita hard. How awfully Palash had pronounced the word! The word seemed to bubble up through a frothy mass of scum floating in a dirty ditch.

"Must you talk like that?"

"Well, I'm being forced to. You're lucky to be able to laze around at home and weep away at leisure. But I have to face the world and all the dirty talk! Forget home and family. What about my office? Friends? Everybody is melting with sympathy. And asking dirty questions."

Romita's voice trembled, "What have they been asking?"

"They have been asking what exactly 'outraging of modesty' implies. What is the difference between 'rape' and 'molestation.'" Palash grit his teeth. "And the language those damned newspapers use! Molestation! Outrage of modesty! Our deputy chief has been trying to find out whether the incident can be termed a rape. As though I'm trying to cover up and pass off rape as an act of molestation!"

"Why? Couldn't you give him a fitting reply?"

"No, I couldn't. I couldn't possibly argue in office about whether my wife had been molested or raped, and to what extent! No sensible husband can do that!"

Romita's ears burned. Palash had actually suppressed all his resentment for seven whole days, been polite and understanding! Given her shade and shelter like a responsible, caring husband. Romita had missed the angry rumblings in the innermost layers of Palash's heart, even though she shared a bed with him!

For the very first time – seven days after the incident, Romita felt slightly guilty even though she had not committed any crime.

Palash remained silent, absently pulling at the roots of his hair. Romita felt for his hand. "Please try not to be so narrowminded."

"Well, my mind isn't a dough of flour that I'll cut it to a perfect shape and size!" Palash snapped back. "Would you like to hear more of what people have been saying? They've been asking whether you knew those men."

A haze of mist descended upon Romita's eyes even as the

scorching summer heat blazed outside, "What do you mean?"

"This means whether you had a ..er ... some sort of an affair with those men before marriage. There were other women at the station as well. Why didn't they target them? Why did they go for *you*, in particular? Why not that Srobona, for instance?"

A gusty wind blew across the balcony after a long lapse. It played around the chairs for some time and died down. Romita's voice broke as she managed to say,"Is that what you believe too? That I knew those men?"

"How can I be sure? How much do I know of your life before our marriage?"

~

Romita stopped short of her bed, which was clean and ready for the night. The rest of the family – her parents-in-law, sister-in-law, brother-in-law – sat engrossed in the lounge, in front of the television. Romita turned back and walked over to her dressing table, to look at herself in the pretty cane-framed oval mirror. But whose face was this, reflected on the neon-lit surface? Was this Romita? Dark circles under the large, thickly-lashed eyes, darkish patches on the glowing, apple-blossom complexion, her shell-white, satin-smooth skin all dry and flaky, drained of colour. Romita picked up a bottle of cleansing milk and some cotton wool absentmindedly. She hadn't stepped out of the house in the last few days, but there was quite a bit of grime hidden in the pores of her skin. The white cotton wool instantly turned black.

Romita returned to her bed after washing her face. The fashionable low 'English' bed – part of her wedding trousseau – had a special built-in box at its head. She opened the box and carefully took out a piece of paper – a few days old newspaper cutting. It had a clear, sharp portrait of Srobona Sarkar in the lower half of the front page.

She examined the face carefully, bringing it as close as possible. The girl was not exactly a beauty, but pretty enough, soft-featured. How on earth could this girl fight those toughs that day? And she was the one who got hurt!

Romita was about to run her fingers lovingly across the photograph, when suddenly alert, she put it back in the box. Palash was entering the room.

He locked the bedroom door and lit a cigarette. He threw a quick glance at Romita. She didn't speak but pulled her pillow closer to the wall and lay down, starting every now and then at the sound of her heart beating furiously. She guessed that Palash hadn't finished his cigarette. He had stubbed it off after a couple of drags and sat down on the bed. Suddenly, leaning forward, he put his arms round Romita, "I'm sorry Rumu," he said. "I didn't mean what I said. Couldn't control my temper and stop myself from saying those words – They seem to rush out."

Romita lay inert. She bit her lower lip hard to control her emotions. Palash pulled her closer to him. Romita's eyes were wet. She threw herself on Palash's chest, sobbing all the while. "Why do all of you hold *me* responsible? What did I do?"

Palash put off the bright light. A few moments of darkness.

Then the room was aglow with a soft blue light from the night lamp. Running his fingers through Romita's thick dark hair, he said, "Tell me, what else could I have done? Ma said, 'We give total freedom to Romita in matters like clothes, shopping, movies. But shouldn't she have consulted us before reporting the incident at the police station and lodging a complaint? She should have at least thought about us!' I tried explaining to Ma that it wasn't you but that girl, who had dragged us to the thana – but Ma wouldn't believe me. Actually Ma is helpless too ... With the leaders of the Mahila Samity* breathing down her neck ... once they get the green signal, they'll just take off – demonstrate in front of the thana, scream their voices hoarse, put up vulgar posters. And the newswallahs will get their juicy stuff once again. Unbearable! Ma has somehow managed to pacify the Samitywalis through Mejomashi, but what about the rest? It was just the other day that Phoolkakima got a chance to pass a comment on your backless choli. Do you know why Baba is so angry? Because we had deposited your torn blouse at the thana."

"But what could I have done? They said that was the rule."

"You simply slipped off to the O.C.'s quarters and came back wearing his daughter's blouse. A housewife from a respectable family should have had some sense of self-respect."

Romita wiped her eyes, "You were there too. Why didn't you stop me?"

"I had lost my head. Besides, in that situation, how could I possibly tell you anything regarding your blouse, especially in the

---

*Mahila Samity: Womens' organizations

presence of an unknown girl?"

"You could have called me elsewhere and told me."

"Told who? Were you in your senses then? Stuck to that girl all the while ... the lawyers will put up that blouse on show in court. Understand? Exhibit number one ..."

Romita became subdued. Darkness had entered through the open window, crouching in surreptitiously. Palash leaned on his elbow and turned to face Romita, "You can't imagine how insulted I felt at the thana today. Of the four boys arrested, only one seemed to be a professional criminal. The rest belonged to respectable homes. Well-to-do families. They were also waiting at the police station. I had to identify those boys in their presence ... it would have been far easier had they belonged to the slums and been pure criminals. This was like identifying our own selves!"

Droplets of sweat formed on Romita's forehead and neck. Wasn't the ceiling fan overhead running at full speed? Romita managed to mumble, "I don't quite follow what you mean."

Palash tried his best to remain calm. "You don't follow a lot of things, Rumu. You don't anticipate how your relatives may react if they see you in a state of nervous breakdown. The way your father kept looking at me while he was visiting you ... As if I wasn't fit to give his daughter any protection."

"I'm sure Baba and Ma never meant it that way. Their mental condition ..." Romita countered feebly.

Palash turned his back to her, "Not all things need to be spelt out in black and white. Facial expressions often give away a person's feelings."

Romita felt the surge of anger coming back, "You didn't you breathe a word about these things in the past seven days? Why raise these topics now? Is it because you had to visit the thana?"

"I suppose it is. Men from respectable homes don't enjoy visiting the thana every day, or for that matter, repeating the same old statements to the police."

"Not even when you have a valid reason for doing so?"

Palash stretched his hand and pulled out a packet of cigarettes from the side table. Romita flung a taunt at him, "Perhaps you felt uneasy in the presence of Srobona Sarkar. Probably, the very thought that the girl had saved your wife – something which you failed to do – hurt your ego."

Palash lit his match, striking it hard, "Good! I see you're talking a lot these days, eh! Drawing inspiration from that picture of the Rani of Jhansi,[*] I believe? Huh, brave woman, my foot! Doesn't possess the minimum feminine dignity. She advised the police to stress upon the kidnapping charge!"

What was feminine dignity? A woman's dignity? Or was it the dignity of being a woman? Romita could see Srobona right in front of her eyes. Flinging her heavy bag crazily at a pack of animals!

Romita suddenly flared up, "Was she wrong? Of course they wanted to kidnap me. Didn't they try to force me down on their motorcycle and drive off?"

Palash's eyes turned vicious, "Oh, it's going to be fun if the

---

[*]Rani of Jhansi, the ruler of a small central Indian kingdom, faught against the British during 1857 Mutiny.

police file the kidnapping case, won't it? Your ditched lovers forcibly carrying you off ..."

"I hate you. The look on your face makes me feel sick! Shame on you!" Romita's voice broke into a wail.

"Oh, you do?" Palash rubbed his cigarette stub hard on the ashtray. He clutched on to Romita's shoulders, his nails biting into her flesh,"Do you want to imagine yourself eloping with those boys?"

"Don't! Don't you touch me! Leave me alone! Let me go!"

"You haven't forgotten the touch of those boys, have you?" Palash's voice was as cruel as a killer's. He crushed Romita's defence with the crazy, blind force of an elephant in heat. Gradually, drained of all strength Romita became limp. Palash forced himself upon her body that lay lifeless like a charred piece of log, flooding it with his virility. He muttered to himself in a fit of rage, "Let me see which Srobona Sarkar protects you now."

There was no moon in the sky. The street lamps had also been put off long since. The pitch darkness of a moonless night enveloped the earth. The universe slept peacefully, as if under an occult spell. Man slept too, exhausted after a display of his own powers. But Romita lay wide-awake.

Suddenly, the raucous voice of a wandering drunk ripped the darkness of the night, "Hey, s-saala darkness, you're trying to frighten me?" his voice slurred. "Am I a lily-livered coward? Get lost. Get out of my sight. Go!"

Romita silently reached out for the box at the head of the bed.

Chapter
Six

*T*he public prosecutor raced through the case diary, his voice monotonous like a mail train. Jhinuk couldn't follow a word. She looked again and again at the dock. Those four – unshaven, hair all rumpled, were up in the dock, after a two-week stint in the police lock-up. They hoped to get bail soon. Three of the Romeos stood with their heads hanging. The fourth's roving eyes sized up the courtroom, alighted on Jhinuk and remained fixed on her. Those were the eyes of a cold-blooded murderer. Jhinuk's blood ran cold. Nobody knew at home that she had come. Perhaps she should have stayed away today.

Three men in expensive suits and ties sat as still as statues, on the bench in front. One whispered to the bald, old lawyer in the first row of benches. The atmosphere was tense, full of suspense.

The room had once served as a stable for horses during the

British rule. The high, dank ceiling had plaster peeling off in large flakes. It could cave in any moment. The plaster and paint on the walls were peeling off too. They hadn't seen a paintbrush since the country's independence. The dull, fading walls absorbed all the light from the bulbs. An ancient ceiling fan droned overhead, spreading a disgusting musty smell all around. The judicial bench was covered with a piece of red cloth. The wooden plank, the chairs, tables and the dock. A film of dust lay on every piece of furniture in the room.

Seated a little high up, on a chair that was comparatively less dirty, was the sub-divisional judicial magistrate. Apart from a police officer, there were a couple of emaciated looking constables who stood on guard near the door. The unruly mob outside couldn't get past them and enter the courtroom. There was no similarity between this courtroom and the ones created on movie or television sets. Jhinuk looked up startled, as a deep voice spoke. The bald old lawyer from the front bench had stood up.

"Your Honour," he said. "The case diary and my learned public prosecutor's opinion admit the fact that the four accused belong to distinguished, well-to-do families. First accused, Partha Sikdar, happens to be the son of a well-known physician, Dr. Nihar Sikdar. Second accused Suman Halder's father Bidesh Halder is a top-ranking government official. Rakesh Gupta, alias Ricky's father Radheshyam Gupta is a renowned construction merchant."

"Construction merchant! What stops him from calling the man a building promoter?" Jhinuk didn't pay much heed to Sharat. She continued to chew her bubblegum hard, her ears picking up every word the lawyer uttered.

"Fourth accused Badal Chatterjee, alias Laata, is an orphan from a poor family," the lawyer continued. "First, second and third accused are all second year students from a respectable college – one of the best in the city. The fourth is a close friend of these three. Badal Chattejee's father, late Bankim Chatterjee taught Bengali at Ramratan High School. Boys hailing from such respectable families can never commit such a heinous crime. The police are simply trying to destroy the social status and goodwill the families enjoy by involving them in false cases."

"The accused have been identified at the thana, sir. And there's a criminal record against Badal Chatterjee," pleaded the public prosecutor.

The bald man smiled. "It seems that our learned prosecutor has forgotten a few simple facts. Number one, identification at the thana has no legal validity whatsoever, and number two, none of their names had been mentioned in the F.I.R. Therefore, there is no point in further investigations, is there? Number three, whether Sections 354, 363 and 509 of the Indian Penal Code can be applied in this case is still debatable and under legal consideration. Fourth, there is no proven criminal record against Badal Chatterjee. Please note, Your Honour, no proven criminal record. Finally, if at all, the accused are considered to be suspects, the court may consider granting them bail keeping in mind their social background."

By this time, the public prosecutor's voice had risen too, "No Sir," he said. "I strongly oppose the bail, more so in view of their respectable family backgrounds. Those of us who enjoy a fair amount of social goodwill and status should have a stronger sense of social responsibility as well. The offence for which they have been arrested is a crime committed not only against a woman but against society as a whole."

Jhinuk, by this time, felt a touch of excitement and brightened up. "Thank God," she said to herself. "No chance of their being bailed out today."

Sharat leaned towards Jhinuk. "No, they'll get it. Didn't you hear the police report?"

"Not really ... the gentleman read it so fast ..."

"The police claim that *prima facie* investigations are over. There's no need for police custody. If the court wants, the accused can be sent to judicial custody. Is there any hope of stopping them from getting the bail after this?"

Sharat Ghoshal was right. All four were soon released on private bails. The court ordered the police to frame a charge sheet within ninety days. Meanwhile, the accused could not leave town without the court's permission.

Jhinuk felt depressed. The four ruffians would walk out free in front of her eyes! They would roam the city streets without a care, like any other normal, honest citizen. Nobody would realize that these four boys, moving about everywhere, were the same who had committed a terrible crime! Bother! It would have been better if she hadn't come to court today. Jhinuk poured out her anguish and dissatisfaction outside, standing under a banyan tree, "It's the police. It's only because of them that those fellows are out on bail."

Sharat laughed heartily. "Oh no," he said. "They would have got the bail anyway. The police were just an excuse!"

"Of course not," Jhinuk argued. "I've noticed that the police have consistently refused to stress the kidnapping charge, since the day they filed the diary."

"Why do you think so? The section *has* been included in the report! It's too early to think about the chargesheet now. Even if the point is included in the chargesheet, Robinda will have a hard time trying to prove it."

"Why? The motive is clear."

"Motives will simply be swept away by the pressures of power and social influence, madam. Do you know how powerful that Nihar Sikdar is? Several ministers are his regular patients. For that matter, his son would never have been arrested had the papers not been out with the story in such great detail."

Clouds had gathered in the sky; the sun had disappeared behind them. Yet the bricks, the cement and the wood of the building let off heat. Two Marutis and an Ambassador were parked at a distance. The three men in formal suits stood next to the cars. The three respectable gentlemen! Jhinuk stood defiantly, with her back to them.

Sharat Ghoshal called out to her, "Come this way. Would you care for some tea?"

Jhinuk and Sharat hardly knew each other. She had met him at her grandmother's old age home, Shantiparabar. She remembered having a long chat with him one day in Thamma's room. But did that mean they were close enough to have tea together?

Jhinuk turned down the offer. "Not today, thanks," she said. "I plan to visit the University's Alipore campus now."

"How can I allow that? If Mrinalma comes to know that I have let you go without getting you a drink, she'll chop me alive!"

"Look, Thamma can never do that. She's not so hot tempered."

"Isn't she? My goodness!" Sharat screwed up his face comically. "Mrinalma can yell at you with her eyes!"

"What!"

"There's the rumble of thunder in her look. It's not just the look. It's a...a... I mean ... you must have noticed the beautiful, bold eyes of goddess Mahisasuramardini*?

Jhinuk approved of the simile. It was a perfect description for Mrinalini. But there were streaks of deep sorrow too, concealed somewhere in that face. It resembled the glossy painted faces of the Durga idols on the day of bisarjan.**

Shanty shops selling tea and sweets had mushroomed all around the open compound. A wide variety of people from different walks of life drank tea and chatted inside the dingy shops. Their postures spelt a strange kind of secretiveness.

Jhinuk sat down on a long, narrow bench, next to Sharat.

"You're quite amazing. I am surprised!"

"Why? Is it because I earn my bread here? Was that rather unexpected?"

"A homeopath doctor attached to an old age home is also a practising lawyer at the Alipore Police Court! It's unbelievable!"

---

*Mahisasuramardini is another name for the goddess Durga.

**Bisarjan is the immersion of the idol.

Sharat's thick lips spread into a smile. "Homeopathy is my passion," he explained. "And this happens to be my job. Nothing clandestine about that, but it is not the kind of job that one can boast of."

Jhinuk shook her head. "Thank god I met you this morning! I have never been to the court before! Couldn't follow a thing! It is just a crazy medley of typewriters, black coats and endless human heads. Everybody is rushing around for no particular reason! It is just like those fast forward scenes in the movies."

"Hum. This is a queer place no doubt. Everyone is busy. Men of business."

"You're calling lawyers businessmen?"

"You've caught on quick. Yes, this is definitely a business centre. A place for making money. Catch hold of clients and squash them flat under thick, heavy law books. But fifty per cent of the people you see here have no work. Even those black-coated penguins that you see, are the same."

Sharat Ghoshal sported a white, full-sleeved shirt, even in the height of summer heat. The shirt was buttoned up to his neck. Sharat loosened his collar and relaxed, "Some of these people have been driven to this place by curiosity alone – like you."

"Actually, I had some work to finish at the university's Alipore campus, which is quite close by. Since I was coming so far, and I knew those men had been arrested, I thought I would just peep in and check out on the proceedings myself."

"Good decision." Sharat turned his wrist, and peered through his cuff to look at his watch.

"Well, I got a chance to see the four Romeos and their parents as well, courtesy you! There was a huge crowd the previous day! All because of the news being flashed in the papers. There isn't much of a crowd today!"

"This city has a short memory! It doesn't remember much madam, gets over-excited about a new issue, and forgets it the very next day. *You* might not remember much about the case after three months."

"You mean the case won't be put up in the next three months?"

"Nope! You might as well settle down and have a good sleep. The police will look for more witnesses, record their statements and then plan the case. There are thousands of formalities in the procedure."

Tea and sweets had meanwhile arrived. Jhinuk picked up her cup with a depressed look on her face. "You mean the case will go into temporary hibernation?"

"Everything won't be rolled up. The magistrate seems to be strict enough. The chargesheet will be submitted within ninety days. Then watch out for the game to start. Witnesses won't turn up on time; their lawyers will take up some of their appointment dates. If the accused are convicted here, they still have the District Court, the High Court and finally the Supreme Court to appeal to."

"But the fact that the girl suffered extreme humiliation, what about the solution to ..." Jhinuk put down her tea cup,"Is nobody going to give a thought to her shame? Is nothing going to be done about that?"

"The law is blindfolded madam. It has no emotion. Look at the Archana Guha* case! Fifteen years have passed. Has anybody been punished? If there is a conviction in your case, do you think Mr. Sikdar and Guptaji will leave it at that? You'll probably see this case being stretched so long that the victim will become a grandmother by the time it ends – Provided the case proceeds that far!"

Jhinuk felt a deep darkness engulf her. Her protest had no importance, no consequence at all! The whole thing appeared absurd. The sum total of all her courage and protest was ... zero!

Sharat perhaps read Jhinuk's thoughts. He laughed,"Are you upset? This is only the trial procedure, There's another side to it. You look as though you're mentally involved in the case. But can you guarantee that the victim is also thinking like you?"

Jhinuk faced a dilemma. Romita's mother-in-law had been curt with her over the phone. Even Palash seemed to withdraw like a snail going into its shell when he had met her at the police station. He had looked impatient and irritated.

Jhinuk mumbled,"Won't the girl think of her own honour and dignity?"

"Good if she does!" Sharat managed to fish out his snuff box

---

*Archana Guha's case during the Naxalite movement was a high profile case in West Bengal; she was tortured in police custody.

from his trouser pocket. Tapping his forefinger on the lid of the box, he said, "The way you look, I doubt whether your own patience will last out!"

Jhinuk blushed. What did this man think she was? Would she lose her enthusiasm so soon? Sharat Ghoshal didn't know her well enough. He didn't know that Jhinuk wasn't the type to give up so easily and accept defeat. Whatever she began, she pursued till she saw the end of it.

As a fresher in college, she had refused to subscribe to the students' union. She had argued, "Our views aren't compatible. So why should I become a member?" One of the union boys had abused her. But Jhinuk hadn't let him off easily. She lodged a complaint against the boy at the union office. They didn't pay much heed, and asked her to go and report the incident to the principal. The principal in turn had shrugged and said, "Goodness! I would stay away from student politics. This is a minor affair, best shrugged off." But Jhinuk was not to be discouraged. She reported the incident to the local party office, once again without much success. The district office listened to her entire story carefully, but later suppressed it, mouthing the usual excuse, "Let's see what can be done." Jhinuk had moved straight on to the state committee office. "Do something. Or else, I'll flash it in the papers!" she had threatened. Finally, the boy had to submit a written apology.

Tunir still pulled her leg about this incident. She now repeated what he had told her," Do you know what my friends have to say about me? They say Jhinuk's clutch is like a turtle's bite, she doesn't let go easily."

Sharat screwed up his eyes and looked at her, "And if that same turtle is turned on its back? You've seen how helpless and miserable it is then, how frantically it throws its legs in the air?" Sharat demonstrated the posture of turned turtles, flailing his arms comically. "Ee-e-e-e," he screeched.

Jhinuk glared at Sharat, "You'll see for yourself whether I have the tenacity to wait."

Sharat took off his brown, thick-framed glasses and wiped them clean with his handkerchief. "Don't take my words too seriously. I said it on an impulse. We actually try to match people with our experiences, don't we? Initially, each person appears to be slightly different from the rest. Later, they all begin to resemble one another. Does man ever venture to step out of his enclosure unless he has been hit hard?"

Sharat's voice was so intense and sincere that the indignation Jhinuk had felt within herself lessened considerably. Hadn't the man said something similar, sitting in Mrinalini's room? However much people tended to be overwhelmed by anger, jealousy, fear or grief, basic human nature underwent little change. And with the help of a handful of primary human characteristics and qualities, it was fairly easy to identify and assess individuals accurately.

Jhinuk said in a light vein, "That's your old theory! The three primary elements in human nature – goodness; spiritedness; ignorance and vice!"

Sharat burst into laughter. "No, that's not right. Arthritis. Phlegm, and Bile. Man can't escape these three. That's a quote from Herr Hahnemann."

"But didn't you say something entirely different the other day?"

"It's the same thing. There are always two sides to a coin. But does the coin change if you turn it around? I always speak out contrarily at every situation. When I examine a patient, I keep his character and nature in mind, while in court I look out for my client's physical condition. That's all. Half my work is done!"

Jhinuk screwed up her nose in mock anger. "Oh! Now I see why the inmates of Shantiparabar — Thamma's Home—are never cured of any disease."

"Did you think I was actually a medical doctor? Goodness! I don't visit Shantiparabar to cure diseases! I visit them for long chats. And truly speaking…" Sharat lowered his voice as if disclosing top military secrets, "They have just one disease that can never be cured!"

"What's the disease? They're highly eccentric, aren't they?"

"No. They are lonely. Totally lonely."

Jhinuk's heart missed a beat. The more she watched Sharat Ghoshal, the more amazed she was. He could weave a magic spell around people with his chatter. No wonder the old ladies of Shantiparabar were so fond of Sharat, the doctor!

Jhinuk suddenly noticed the man's eyes; they were jet black. Human eyes normally weren't so black.

Sharat glanced at his watch again.

Jhinuk sounded embarrassed, "I think I've kept you waiting

too long. You're late!"

"No. I have a case in the second half of the session at two."

"Do you like the job at the court? You could open a doctor's chamber instead, couldn't you?"

"The thrill here is of a special kind, madam. It's very different. Providing courage and support to an otherwise fit person suffering helplessly from mental trauma ... the case I have today is very interesting. A woman visited her former husband, asking for alimony. That wonderful husband of hers beat her black and blue. He also stripped her in public."

Jhinuk shivered in disgust. "And then?"

"Well, nothing after that. That saint of a man has now been set free on bail. And the woman has been falling at my feet, requesting me to wind up the criminal case lodged against him, hoping that the man would then probably give her some money out of sheer pity."

"But the woman forgot her humiliation?"

"Does the stomach come first or dishonour?" Sharat sounded slightly irritated. "This is the mistake that we, middle class people, often make. We start thinking of a girl's honour and the purity of her body at the very outset. You see, men attach honour to a woman's body when it suits their need. And they strip the same woman when they need to!"

Jhinuk looked glumly at him, "You mean women's physical purity has no real value?"

"There's value if we males want it. There's no value when we don't. Do you know what chastity is, madam? Ensuring that the son that's being born to me is actually mine. I mean, I have to see to it that I am actually the child's father. And chastity is the weapon. Only we men execute that weapon. I wouldn't tolerate a young cuckoo intruding into my nest for instance, enjoying the fruits of labour."

"You mean to say that ownership rights alone give birth to the concept of chastity?"

"Goodness! I wouldn't be able to discuss such high-sounding philosophy! I just know that 'chastity' and 'honesty' are synonymous. Much like the two sides of a coin. Remaining honest to one's own self is chastity. Be it men or women."

His words didn't quite match Jhinuk's beliefs; still she listened to him, fascinated. She tried arguing now, "In that case, wouldn't you agree that the humiliation inflicted upon Romita Choudhuri was not shameful?"

"It was dishonour certainly. Hurting someone mentally or physically against that person's wish, definitely is. The act should be condemned and the accused punished. If a mad dog bites you on the road, should we let that dog go free?"

Jhinuk said inwardly, "Ah mister! Aren't you sensitive! A little hurt to someone and your eyes fill with tears!" Outwardly she hurriedly said, "Let's go. The staff room at the campus will be locked up soon."

Jhinuk glanced once again at Sharat, while coming out of the teashop. A young woman of about thirty was speaking to him. She had two children with her. One was in her arms, clinging to her. Sharat Ghoshal spoke to the woman with his eyes closed.

The woman had sindoor smeared thickly down the parting of her hair, a big dot of sindoor showed on her forehead. Her hands were full of red and white bangles married women wore.

Was this the woman who was beaten up by her husband who never gave her alimony? Was this the woman?… Was she? …Oh the poor woman!

Would Romita Choudhuri turn out to be like her?

Chapter Seven

A small storm rose in the evening – erratic sweeps of dust followed by a few large blobs of rain. The blaze of midsummer heat had somewhat cooled.

Jhinuk picked up a dry twig from the pavement and hit Tunir lightly on his back. "Your words have finally come true – feeling great aren't you?"

The road winding past the lake was quiet and pretty. It was lined with trees on both sides: krishnachuda, radhachuda, simul, sirish. The wide boulevard was tinged with a glowing shimmer of green. The lake lay to the left. The lakeside was quite crowded in the summer evening. Only a few people walked along the pavement opposite, even though it hadn't yet become dark.

Tunir was smiling, "Shouldn't I be amused? I keep visualizing the court scene. Those four chaps glaring at you from the dock.

Glaring at you and dying of shame, after the sound bashing they received from a five-footer girl that left them almost dead!"

"I'm not a five-footer. I'm five feet and an inch!"

"That hardly makes a difference."

Light filtered in through the dense foliage. A silent stream of traffic flowed down the road. With sudden flashes of light, the yellow flowers of the radhachuda smiled in the dark.

"Ma has asked you to come over one of these days," said Tunir.

"Why?"

"Might give you toffees. Women have tremendous unity in these matters. One woman shows a sudden spurt of courage and the whole lot swells with pride. Didi has been making daily trips from Moulali to Dhakuria, to sing your praise. 'You needn't worry Tunai. You'll have Jhinuk to protect you after you get married. If you're ever assaulted on the road, you'll just have to send a word across, and Jhinuk will take care of it."

"Tanimadi's words have been stinging you, right? Jealous?"

"Of course not. Women are genetically cowards. A couple of slightly brave ones might suddenly show courage... Don't you know that story? A man accidentally tumbles into the ocean from a ship. Everybody stands aghast on the deck, nobody tries saving him. Suddenly, someone dives in. The two somehow manage to scramble up to the ship's deck. The captain, crew and the passengers hail the saviour, praising his guts. But the man fumes with rage and glares at everybody. He blurts out finally, "Stop that nonsense! Tell me, which one of you pushed me into the sea?"

"That's a poor joke. An old one."

"You don't know the end of the story. That wasn't actually a man. The person was later found to be a woman. By the way, did you see who pushed *you* to the frontline that day?"

"I warn you. Get off my back! Remember how I had bashed you up? Shall I bash you up once again?" Jhinuk began to laugh.

They were in college then. Tunir Majumdar of third year commerce had entered the first year political science classroom with his mates, for a session of mandatory ragging.

He had faced Jhinuk, "You've been fighting a duel with the students' union from day one, eh? Giving them a tough time. What guts! Good! I like it. Do you like me?"

"You're not too bad, will do." Unsuspecting, Jhinuk had rapped back smartly.

"In that case, imagine I'm Amitabh Bachchan and you're Rekha. Make love to me."

Jhinuk had frozen. Was this ragging? It was vulgar and crossed all limits of civility!

"Come on, start." His bronze body in perfect shape, without an extra inch of flab, Tunir had pretended to strike a pose.

Jhinuk had stood like a wild, stubborn filly, "I can't."

"What do you mean, you can't?" A girl from the group had demanded sharply.

"I mean I can't. That's all!"

"Then what can you do for us, baby? Can you fight?"

"Do anything, stupid! They won't let you go if you don't,"

Bishakha had whispered into her ears.

Jhinuk was glowing like a furnace in anger and humiliation. Glaring back, she had retorted, "I can do whatever I like, right? To this Amitabh Bachchan?"

She had sent a swinging blow at Tunir's stomach and had violently pulled at his hair; and she had continued to pummel him crazily on his chest and back.

"What do you think you're doing? My god! Has this girl gone crazy?" Eight to ten hands tried dragging Jhinuk away. But she had stood her ground, determined not to budge. Her hands had moved like a pair of pistons. And the big-built five feet eleven inch Tunir had nearly fallen flat at this sudden assault. Clutching his stomach, he had stooped low, gasping for breath. But with a bright smile on his lips.

Jhinuk had never been cool and collected after this incident. Her blood boiled if she met Tunir during those days. But a single brush with jaundice had reversed the picture!

That happened before she moved on to the second year of college. Their summer holidays had begun. Tunir's graduation exams were just over and he belonged to the batch of outgoing students.

He had turned up at Jhinuk's house all of a sudden, one hot summer afternoon looking foolishly apologetic and tense. Jhinuk was in bed with jaundice. He didn't have much to say except hand her the huge pompelmoose he had brought. It was supposed to be particularly good for jaundice, he claimed. On the second day, he carried a long stick of sugarcane. Sugarcane juice was good for jaundice patients, he insisted. On the third day, he fished out a string of beads from his pocket. It was supposed to be a herbal cure for jaundice; the patient had to wear it round the neck during the period of illness.

Sujata's heart melted before Jhinuk's did. Sujata waited out in the balcony on the fourth day, expecting 'that boy' to turn up any moment. As Tunir rang the doorbell, a thousand African Masai drums beat in Jhinuk's heart. What would the boy bring her today!

He did bring her something. Warm smiles. Smiles that would melt a stony heart. Smiles that could create a verdant oasis, an evergreen forest, in the midst of the Gobi and the Sahara. It was hardly surprising that the smiles swept Jhinuk off her feet!

That was just the beginning. For six years Tunir had seeped into Jhinuk's bones, veins and nerves, drop by drop.

Jhinuk's voice broke as she spoke, "Do you remember?"

"What?"

"Those days."

Tunir remained silent and held on to Jhinuk's hand passionately. At times, silence can be so vocal! During these quiet moments, even the work-crazy Tunir metamorphosed into a warm, lovelorn youth – an enchanting young hunter walking the forests of an ancient land. These moments were timeless, without a past, or a future. The silent walk together was the only reality, an endless present without a beginning or an end!

"I feel fatigued these days," Jhinuk said.

Tunir pressed her hand, "Why?"

"I don't know."

Jhinuk's body trembled like a wounded doe's. "I feel extremely depressed and out of sorts when I'm all by myself, I wake up with a nagging pain. If I happen to doze off in the afternoon, layers of hurt overpower me. But I can't locate the reason. Nothing attracts me – the world goes gray. I can't stand any kind of sound – not even the voices of people talking. Not the TV. Not friends. Nothing."

"Not me either?"

Jhinuk held back a sigh. "How do I reach you then? You're in office, glued to your seat, in front of the computer!"

Tunir pulled Jhinuk closer to himself, "You've never told me about this before. This is a dangerous disease. It's called 'afternoonitis'!"

"What did you say?"

"'Afternoonitis'. It's a very serious type of allergy. If the virus of 'loveria' happens to be present in the body…"

Jhinuk pinched Tunir's hand, "Don't pull my leg!"

"I'm not. There's just one cure for this allergy. Marriage. The only diet – Honeymoon! There are certain specific medicines, rules and conditions for treatment as well. You'll need lonely mountains. A bungalow with glass windows. Daylong snowfall. Fireplace warming up chilly afternoons. And just you and me in the room. Me and you. You need about seven such afternoons. The deadly allergy is sure to vanish into thin air."

Jhinuk pinched him once again, harder this time.

"No, I'm serious. Sanyal in my office is getting married in July. He's a year junior to me but he'll soon achieve seniority by being married!"

"Who has asked you to be a junior? Ma has been after you, hoping and planning since ... it's you who have been acting evasive and postponing it. Tanimadi mentioned it too ..."

"Do you think I enjoy putting it off? It is not wise to marry before I'm able to secure a firm foothold on the corporate ladder. Moreover, there is virtually a tug-of-war in office about the trip abroad."

"But you said they will send only a computer-trained person. Your Kuruvilla doesn't have computer training!"

"*Doesn't have* is only half the truth. You should talk in the past tense and say *he didn't have*. Kuruvilla is taking a crash course at an American software institute at the moment, spending twenty-two thousand. Can you imagine? Twenty-two thousand bucks!"

"So what? Won't your company value your hard work, your seniority?"

"Hard work isn't the only password. The game is to put up a public show of hard work. Kuruvilla is an expert in this." Tunir's lips twisted in mockery, "He has mastered the art of pressing the correct switches and activating the bosses."

The boulevard was lined with tall, beautiful skyscrapers. Nearly every apartment sparkled with bright rays of light. A few windows were mysteriously dark.

Jhinuk tried consoling him, "You have the calibre. You can always leave this job and find some other, if things are that bad."

"Tunir Majumdar isn't the kind of guy to give up and quit so easily," Tunir declared, but without much conviction. He added with a light humour, "You'll never get to know a man's world. If only you realised how tough the battle is!"

"Your Neelam knows it well enough, doesn't she?"

Tunir let go off Jhinuk's hand. Neelam was a Punjabi girl. She had recently joined Tunir's office. They both shared the same cubicle. Neelam's chartered accountancy exam results were better than Tunir's. She had recently got married and changed her surname from a Punjabi Malhotra to a Bengali Dasgupta.

"Why did you stop talking?"

Tunir was in a sombre mood. "Neelam made three mistakes in the statement today. If I hadn't pointed them out to her, the finance director would have summoned her. She's often excused simply because she's a woman."

Jhinuk was amused. Whenever Neelam's name cropped up, Tunir would start drawing up a list of her flaws to prove how inefficient she was. He never missed a single opportunity.

There was a sizeable crowd in front of Safari Park. With evening settling in, it was party time, with street vendors scattered around a long line of parked cars, offering a variety of savouries – phuchkas, bhelpuris and jhalmuris. A young boy carried a portable stove with a boiling pot of tea on it. Tunir stopped him and ordered two earthen cups of tea.

"Chhoton inquired about you today. It seems you've promised to treat him to prawn cocktail?"

"Yeah, next month. Let Babua be back. Why only the two of them! I shall treat Mashima as well."

Jhinuk pinched Tunir once again. She wanted to put Tunir's

mood back to its normal rhythm. "Are you going to call my mother Mashima even after we get married? Will you still use *tui* while talking to me?"

"Well, you do that too."

"I'll change overnight."

"Women can and women must, but I can't change myself overnight." Eyes twinkling with laughter, his face serious, Tunir said, "The question doesn't arise before the honeymoon is over."

Jhinuk pinched him once again. It was so hard this time that Tunir winced aloud in pain. Several heads from the crowd turned to look at them. Embarrassed, Jhinuk walked fast along the pavement ahead of Tunir.

"I forgot to ask you, Jhinuk. Did that couple go to court?" Tunir had quickly caught up with her.

"No!"

"Not even the husband?"

"Uhuh."

"Do you see now? Remember the old adage, *The bride forgets her wedding date but the neighbours spend sleepless nights?* This man, whose wife was almost kidnapped, spent a relaxed morning lazing at home while you wasted a whole day in court. Moreover, you got a yelling from Mashima and Meshomoshai for going there."

Jhinuk looked crestfallen. At times, her parents could be so difficult! Was it possible to lead a normal life with so much tension and fear in one's mind! Sadly enough, Chhoton had turned out to be the same sort! He would always sing in tune with his parents!

Jhinuk moved closer to Tunir. "I forgot to tell you something I've suddenly remembered. I met someone really interesting in the court. Doctor Sharat. You could call him Lawyer Sharat as well. He practises homeopathy medicine at Thamma's old home. And he also happens to be the government pleader at the Alipore Court. The man comes up with strange theories about people. You should hear him talk… you'll be enchanted!"

"It's part of lawyers' business to talk smart. They trade off words to earn their living," Tunir spoke casually, without paying much heed to the subject.

"It's not like that. You would understand my point if you saw him. He has made me more doggedly determined to fight. He has challenged me to see the end of the case."

Tunir frowned, "Is he a peevish old lawyer?"

Jhinuk smiled inwardly. Tunir was actually trying to find out the man's age. Men didn't like listening to their women praising other men.

Jhinuk played around with her words, "I wouldn't call him old. He could be forty. Could be forty five. I wouldn't be surprised if he turned out to be fifty. Aren't there some people whose looks don't give away their age? Well, it's like that. It's our mind that makes us age or feel young!"

"Oh, you mean he is the weather-beaten type."

"No, I don't. He is small-built. Slim, with a dark but glowing complexion. His eyes are the most attractive part of his looks. If diamonds were coal black …"

"I know. The raven type," Tunir threw a casual banter. "You

had better watch out. Middle-aged men are often sex-starved…'

They turned left at the next turning. The road was comparatively well lit, clearly revealing that half of Tunir's face that now turned to Jhinuk. "Jhinuk, you're highly obsessed with bravado. You should keep in mind that those men are now free."

"So?"

"They have certainly marked you."

"I care two hoots if they have. Let them recover from what the police have fed them with over the last two weeks!"

"You know nothing. The police hardly touch people belonging to wealthy, influential families. They usually manage to get past the police in the lock-up. A note from the Reserve Bank can transform the jail to a five-star hotel."

"It's not that easy. The O.C. seemed to be a stern fellow. I've spoken to him, so I should know." Jhinuk refuted in a firm voice. "They wouldn't have been arrested otherwise."

"You can never tell. Maybe their bartering wasn't successful. Perhaps the uproar in the press compelled the police to take a firm step." Light from the street lamps reflected on Tunir's glasses. "Do you think those boys from powerful, influential families will digest this humiliation quietly? Maybe they are on your track now, this moment!"

Almost instantly, Jhinuk's eyes turned left. A shock wave hit her. There was actually someone walking close to them. A bearded man was at their heels; he walked at the same pace, along the dark lakeside! Was he looking this way?

Jhinuk's feet froze. Her heart hammered. Unconsciously, she

popped a chewing gum into her mouth. She clutched on to Tunir. The man seemed to have stopped too. He now walked slowly up to them.

Jhinuk forgot to chew her gum for a few seconds. Then she realised her mistake. The burly, bearded old man walked slowly past them. He didn't even look back.

Tunir burst out laughing, "You must admit that I wasn't wrong in my theory of the genetic factor! A brave woman like you trembling with fright!"

Jhinuk wanted to laugh heartily. She couldn't.

Tunir's hand rested on Jhinuk's shoulder, "Why are you so nervous? I'm here with you," he soothed her. "Come, look at me, will you!"

Jhinuk breathed heavily. Her ears were burning; she was hardly conscious of it.

Chapter Eight

*J*hinuk was going through the letters – letters that had been redirected from the newspaper office. They had been coming in batches over the last few days – in twos, threes and fives: Debika Kayal from Kakdwip, Manasree Basu from Raiganj, school teacher Amita Bhattacharjee from Kanthi – they all read the same. "We face so much indignity out on the streets everyday, on a bus or train. As our representative, you have taken a firm stand against the shame and dishonour inflicted on us. Your courage is our inspiration ..." There were a few letters from men as well. "Congratulations. Hearty congratulations to you!" While some letters had a distinctly different note. "I would like to meet an extraordinarily brave woman like you. I hope that an independent minded Srobona Sarkar will respond to my invitation…"

Jhinuk tore the last few letters to pieces and threw them out of the window. Bits of paper floated in the air, across the stagnant pool of water; a few got hopelessly stuck in the undergrowth, failing to reach the ground.

Jhinuk stood by the window, preoccupied by the recurrent early morning dream. She had had the same dream thrice in the last seven days. The same house. The same courtyard. The well. Cluster of trees. Music. The coconut tree.

The house resembled their old Charu Market home, with extended balconies on both sides. Sandwiched between were Thamma-Dadu's bedroom, Jhinuk's parents' bedroom and Kakamoni-Kakima's bedroom. But that house in Charu Market didn't have such a large courtyard, or such huge trees and shrubs! Nor a huge well and a toilet made out of wood behind it!

Dim moonlight, enveloped in long, dark shadows crouched in the corner. The door opened and out came a ten-year old girl into that spooky darkness. The severe winter cold clung to her body and chilled her bones. She trembled, not so much from the cold but out of fear. To her, the darkness of the silent night carried all kinds of shapes – of ghosts, of hobgoblins, of snakes and toads. The fear of thieves and robbers with bloodshot eyes. What was perhaps most frightening was the unfamiliar darkness itself.

The ten-year old girl, engulfed in cold and fear, tried running across to the toilet. As soon as she stepped forward… whoosh! The courtyard and the toilet moved further back. And the trees rushed forward, right up to her. Everything went back to place as she scrambled back to the threshold. The girl crept out again; the trees immediately appeared menacingly in front of her! Goodness!

How would she ever reach the toilet? But she had to.

The girl now shut her eyes tight and jumped right into the middle of the quadrangle. The trees and the thickets vanished into thin air, as soon as she landed. There was a void all around her. Only the huge well loomed large, like a big gaping hole in the middle of the enclosure. The girl leaned forward and peered into the well nervously. There was neither water nor darkness in the bottomless pit, but a lion with a ruffled mane sat roaring in the luminous gorge. A song resounded from somewhere, "*Aaj na chhorunga tujhe dum duma dum.*" Sulagna yelled across the room, "Please play that song from *Khalnayak*." Bishakha and Mainak's voices could be heard, "But you can't! The songs have been arrested under TADA." As the little girl looked up from the well, the courtyard, the house at the corner, and the night had all melted into thin air! A tall coconut tree stood taut and erect in the glaring sunlight, flooding the place. It was exactly like the tree that now stood in front of Jhinuk's eyes, next to the pool of muddy water.

What on earth could the dream mean? The girl was ten years old but her face and mind resembled Jhinuk's, as she was now.

Jhinuk could recognize the well, the courtyard and clusters of trees and thickets. It was Simultala. But Jhinuk hadn't been to Simultala as a ten-year old child! When had she gone there? Three years ago perhaps. She had been on this trip with her friends from the university. They had stayed at the sprawling garden house that belonged to Anindita's family. How did that fairy tale lion of her childhood come to sit inside the well? Why the coconut tree? The dream melted away as she woke up. Only the coconut tree remained. Tall and erect like a slender minaret. But why? What did it mean?

Jhinuk had planned to tell Tunir about her dream last evening, but she hadn't. Something had stopped her. She had felt as though Tunir would come to know of her innermost fears. Well, it could be that Jhinuk's distraught mind gave shape to such strange dreams. It was true, she had experienced fear twice over the last few days. Once at the court, watching those murderous eyes and the second time at the lake, with the bearded man. Did fear recur as dreams ...? Did the seed of fear lie deep within the subconscious as an imagined fiend? If that is the truth, then why aren't human minds equipped with the power to destroy such fears as well?

Sounds of loud voices floated out of the kitchen. The thread of thoughts in Jhinuk's mind snapped. It was one of those horrible squabbles between her mother and the maid –Gobindo's Ma.

Sujata gave a shrill cry, "You've finished the detergent in ten days! The washing powder for the dishes lasted just fifteen days! How did you manage to exhaust all the spices before the month was over?"

Jhinuk wrapped a housecoat around her and came up to the door. Chhoton had made a snide comment; Ma's voice reached a pitch,"I shall certainly tell her. Why shouldn't the cooking gas last us twenty days at least? She'll do as she pleases. What does she think of herself? There were ten leftover rotis from dinner last night, she's had all ten of them!"

Gobindo's Ma's voice had reached the highest scale too, "I certainly didn't have ten. I had nine. *You* told me to have leftover rotis for breakfast."

"But won't you set a limit to the amount you eat? So many rotis early in the morning... Who asked you to help yourself to the leftover curry in the fridge?"

"Don't nag me about food early in the morning! We work for food – I earn it. One job less doesn't make a difference – there are ten other homes I work for."

Jhinuk didn't much like Gobindo's Ma. She often took money from Jhinuk but never returned it. Even last month she had borrowed twenty rupees for her son's illness. But the bickering over leftover rotis went too far!

Jhinuk spoke out from her bedroom door, "Will you keep quiet Gobindo's Ma? And Ma, if you can't stand her, please look for another maid and let her go. I don't like these daily fights."

Sujata's mind had by that time wandered away from Gobindo's Ma; her eyes had moved from the kitchen to the V.C.P. inside the wooden cabinet in the lounge. A red dot of light flashed from it. Chhoton had been watching films on the V.C.P late last night. He couldn't manage to watch too many films during the short weekends he spent at home, so he made up for lost time during the summer holidays, devouring films by the dozen, often going to bed without switching off the machine.

Sujata marched in and turned the V.C.P. off. Chhoton couldn't care less. He sat at the dining table poring over the sports pages in the newspaper. Jhinuk came up to her brother, "How do you keep watching these films every day? They are identical, with the same dances, same fights, and the same story line. Two brothers separated at birth; one grows up to be a policeman, the other a criminal. And there's always a group of silly, comic villains!"

"You have cultivated the schoolmarm's image to perfection, Didi!" said Chhoton, lowering his high-powered glasses to his nose, "But you have a heart of gold."

Jhinuk smiled. "Don't try those tricks. Speak out – want some cash?"

"Are you thought-reading these days?"

"How much do you need?"

"Whatever you can give. A hundred, two hundred, three hundred."

"What will you do with so much money?"

"I told you. The Darjeeling trip is next Sunday."

"You've already coaxed Baba to cough up money for the trip!"

"Baba is a little tight on cash now. Baba can catch the next batch of students when the summer holidays are over. He has promised me a thousand rupees though. Still, I need a few hundreds extra in hand."

"You'll spend a thousand bucks on a six-day trip and you want more from me?"

"Cut out that drivel. Tell me, will you, or won't you?"

"I won't. Wasting huge amount of Baba's money…"

"Don't call it a wastage. It's investment," Chhoton shrugged off Jhinuk's comment lightly. "You're the expenditure. Wasteful spending."

"What did you say? How dare you talk like that!"

Jhinuk's voice had risen, Sujata came running. "Now the two

of you have started off again! Jhinuk dear, must you? Your brother comes home for a few days ..."

"Does that give him the licence to say and do whatever he likes? Your son has an abominable tongue."

Chhoton burst into a loud guffaw. "Hey Didi, don't lose your temper. You'll get permanent wrinkles on your forehead if you frown too much. The shape of your face will change. Tunirda might faint when he sees that face – A-a-a-a!"

"Let him," Jhinuk retorted angrily. On seeing her brother's funny face, she broke into a smile.

"Your sister is already wracking the poor boy's nerves," said Sujata, "she starts arguing with him at the drop of a hat."

"Why shouldn't I argue when he is wrong?" Jhinuk retorted. "Are his words sacrosanct?"

"I don't know about that. But Tunir definitely has more practical sense than you do. He understands the pros and cons of a situation much better."

"Understands my foot! I too, have a job. I also, have to be out on the streets; have to keep my eyes and ears open."

"Huh! Comparing yourself with Tunir? He has to deal with a wide variety of people. He holds a responsible post in office, has a wide experience ... your job of teaching those lilliputs is hardly comparable!"

Jhinuk didn't want to add fuel to the flames. Ma was always overwhelmed by the accomplishments of her future son-in-law. Of late, he had earned her mother's deep faith by correctly predicting the release of the four accused boys on bail. Even the slightest criticism would be foolish. How could Jhinuk explain to her mother that she felt the pulse of the entire universe in her tiny world of lilliputs! Each child was a representative of a uniquely different, nuclear family. Parents, a daughter, or a son. The highest limit was two kids. Generally, the nucleus of an atom had a greater number of protons and neutrons. The family nucleus ended at "Hum do hamara do!"*

If she spoke for a few minutes with a child, she could derive a great deal of information about the family. For instance, how much the father earned, whether the mother worked, their marital relationship, the serials they loved to watch on television, whether the father drank, what the parents fought about, when they made love, when there were in a good mood. How easily Baba and Ma would buy goodies for their child, even when the child cried for the moon! How the mother behaved when the father's parents visited their home. Or the father, when the mother's parents came over. And once a child had said in a serious tone, "Baba and Ma are not getting on well, Auntie. I think they'll split."

Did Jhinuk exist outside this circle? Jhinuk tried to be objective. No. Yet, when Jhinuk was a child, there used to be a thin curtain drawn between parents and children. Time was slowly drawing that curtain away. The parents' world was now a part and parcel of the tiny world of their kids – forming a strange and confusing picture. Parents now unabashedly discussed all kinds of topics in front of their children, included their children in adult entertainments with a free mind. This was the current trend in

---

*A popular Family Planning slogan of the 70's meaning 'Two for us two'.

contemporary living. Like little droplets of poison, the prohibited world of the adults seeped into the child's bloodstream. The lives of parents and their children were rather self-centered, limited, circumscribed.

Manas was back from the market. His tall, lean body and face were dripping with perspiration. He had long spells of leisure, now that the summer holidays had begun. Private coaching was on the wane. He didn't have to go to college on certain days, when he was off exam duty. He now spent at least a couple of hours shopping for the household.

Sujata walked away to the kitchen with the vegetables and fish. Manas took off his kurta, placed his glasses on the dining table, cooled off under the fan and called out, "Jhinuk, give me a glass of cold water."

"I've got a hilsa from the market," he announced. "Cook it nicely, with mustard and curd."

"How much did you pay for it?" Jhinuk asked.

"Hundred and twenty rupees. It's a good size. I've bought one and a quarter kg."

Sujata's ears were always alert to every little word uttered. They seemed to move around to catch any sound going around the flat. She called out from the kitchen, "Why did you have to buy such expensive fish?"

"Oh, the ilish is an annual affair. And Chhoton loves it. I've overspent only today. Does it matter?"

"Babua is far more fond of ilish maachh than Chhoton. I shall treat him to it too, when he comes back after the summer holidays."

Jhinuk watched Sujata in amazement. She had always been like this, cruel and selfish at times but extremely loving and caring at other.

Manas glanced nervously at Sujata, "Could I have a cup of tea ..."

"You shouldn't have tea coming in from the terrible heat. The parathas are ready, have your breakfast first."

Manas turned to face Jhinuk. "Have you seen the papers?"

"How could I? Does Chhoton ever finish devouring the papers before ten?"

"Look at the first page."

Jhinuk pulled the newspaper from Chhoton's hands and glanced at the headlines. Another person had been arrested in connection with the explosion at the Bombay Stock Exchange. The Joint Parliamentary Committee probing the Harshad Mehta case had completed another session. The chief minister had called upon the citizens of Calcutta to strive towards making the city clean, beautiful and attractive. A public appeal to Indians to build a temple on the Babri Masjid* complex and to lay the foundation of Ramrajya. One hundred and eighty-three women had been raped at a prison camp in Bosnia.

"Is it the Bosnian news that you want me to read?" Jhinuk asked.

"Oh no. Such things often happen during a war. Look down, to the left. At the Nandipur thana lock-up…"

---

*Babri Masjid, a Mughal stucture, was demolished in December,1992 by members of a right wing political party, from the land they thought belonged to Rama.

Jhinuk read the news. It had been published almost as a snippet. The police had raped a woman prisoner inside the lock up!

Manas lit a cigarette, "You're trying to fight a criminal case relying on police support! When the protector is the devourer!"

"The news is quite terrible," Jhinuk said. "But you certainly can't judge the entire police force by a stray incident like this one, can you Baba?"

"Maybe you shouldn't. But on the other hand, you can. I can vouch that when a common citizen lands in trouble, the police usually does nothing. I tried explaining the hazard of your going to court, but you wouldn't listen. It doesn't occur to you that those boys might get excited when they see you. These are bad days. One thing leads to the another! They might throw an acid bulb at you!"

"You always take the worst view," Sujata interrupted. "Must you say such unlucky things?"

"I'm stating facts. This is the hard reality. I want my daughter to realize that. Surenbabu of the philosophy department told me the other day that a girl in his neighbourhood had filed a complaint against a ruffian of the locality. That boy had chucked an acid bulb at the girl. She was badly burnt. This happened only last week."

Jhinuk was taken aback. "It didn't make it to the papers?"

"Are all news published? The girl's father is powerful. He suppressed the news."

"The girl's father ... But why ...?"

"Do I have to explain such a simple thing to you?" Manas

frowned. "He feared a scandal."

"A scandal?"

"You appear to be extremely worldly-wise. Yet, you don't understand how easily a woman's name can be besmirched."

"That's strange! This was an attempt at murder. Won't her family take any steps? The girl could have died!"

"Death relieves a woman of all suffering," Sujata sighed, "It's more painful to live a life of dishonour."

Why must only women suffer the brunt of unforeseen incidents that are caused by men? What kind of a living being was a woman? Just a mindless, brainless body? A womb?

"Those days are gone Ma," said Jhinuk. "Women *will* protest if men misbehave."

"You have done that. And that's enough! You must stop now. You don't realize the amount of worry grown up girls cause parents."

"You could have told us that you wanted to attend court the other day," said Manas. "Someone would have escorted you to the court."

Chhoton got up and sat down on the sofa to watch a vulgar pop number on MTV. A near-naked female body was disintegrating into fragments by computer magic, and was scattered all over the television screen. Chhoton jumped up from the sofa, "You could have told me. Imagine an Arnold Schwarznegger escorting you safely to the court! Would anybody have the guts to even look at you?"

"Oh come on! With that 22-inch rib cage! Fancy you trying to protect me with that!"

Sujata looked at her son, painfully thin in his shorts. But he was growing hair on his arms, legs and chest! Her face bright with pride she said, "Must you pull his leg? Whatever be his chest size, he is a man after all."

"There's hardly any doubt about that! He has it scrawled across his T-shirt as well – 'I am a man'. Thank God you have it written there. It would have been difficult to recognize you as a human being otherwise."

Chhoton laughed loudly. "What would people have thought of me in that case? Superman?"

"An orang outang! What's that you have dangling from your neck? I've been noticing it for the past few days."

"Can't you see? It's a locket!"

"Wait a minute. Why a locket?"

"Just like that!" Chhoton replied evasively.

"His exam results were poor this term," Sujata explained. "So, a friend prescribed a holy locket."

"I'm sure there's a picture of some holy man – a Baba – inside the locket."

"Why must you talk like that?" said Manas. "There's no harm if he derives mental confidence by wearing the locket."

"There's no harm, I admit. I shouldn't object if someone isn't satisfied with just one Baba and goes about dangling twenty Babas from his neck!"

Chhoton tried to be prompt and witty, "Do you know about the special powers that Phuwababa exercises? He is a spiritual man. You must keep in mind that there is a Spirit working behind this huge galaxy. Many people believe in the existence of the Spirit. Even Einstein did!"

"You had better keep that name out of this conversation," retorted Jhinuk. "Why must you dishonour that great man to account for the supernatural powers of your Phuwababa? You had better admit that you couldn't carry on with life on your own. The question is not about the existence of a Spirit, but that you feel helpless without a protector. How on earth could you protect me in that case?"

"Giving protection is rather difficult these days," declared Manas in a troubled voice. His expression spelt worry too. "Particularly so for middle class people like us," he carried on. "Those of us who are not into politics, who don't have much money and connections, are the most helpless lot. Think of the power those people wield – the people you messed up with! Forget money power. Take that top government official for instance. Doesn't he have connections with the top brass of the police? And promoters are great chums of political leaders! Could the police catch the true offenders behind that mass rape at Birati a few days ago? On the contrary, even the women's committee of the local party declared that those women were at fault as they were of questionable character!"

Jhinuk watched her father carefully. She could clearly sense that these words were not her father's. He had heard them being discussed elsewhere and he was merely repeating them. Keeping her eyes fixed on him, she asked, "Will you answer a question,

Baba? Suppose those boys didn't belong to wealthy, influential homes but hailed from a background like ours or even lower down the social ladder, would you have supported my going to the court?"

Usually, Manas didn't talk much, but when he did, he never stopped before a full forty-five minute lecture. He replied in an exasperated voice, "These are hypothetical questions. Is it possible to forecast the consequences of a imaginary situation?"

Jhinuk was amused. She was sure her parents would have objected even then. Honour! Women's honour was extremely brittle! Even when street ruffians made passes at women, the victims were cautioned and asked to be more careful. It was rather strange! Her father too, never went by logic! Perhaps he didn't want to. Either he suffered from acute tension, or he helplessly succumbed to the circumstances in silence.

Jhinuk tried to reduce her father's fears. "Don't worry too much about my going to court Baba. Sharatbabu said if they cause me the slightest trouble on the road, those boys would be arrested once again. And in that case, nothing on earth would grant them bail."

Meanwhile, Sujata had served Manas his breakfast. Manas tore a piece of paratha, "Which Sharat?" he asked.

"Sharat Ghoshal. I think you've seen him. At Thamma's old people's home."

Manas couldn't remember.

Jhinuk tried to jog his memory. "He is the homeopath doctor at Shantiparabar. Dark and small-built. With a salt-and-pepper moustache."

Chhoton had gone back to the television; he chipped in from

his seat there, "What was he doing in the court? Was he arrested after killing his patients?"

"No. He is the government lawyer at the Alipore court."

"A homeopath lawyer?" Chhoton reverted to his earlier teasing.

"Why are you making fun of him? Can't one attend court and practise homeopathy simultaneously?"

"A government lawyer can certainly do it. He has all the time in the world. Comes to office, leaves for home, earns his pay; gets some extra if he works! Try and find out more about him; I'm sure you'll see that he wasn't doing too well for himself. Must have found the right way to get into the government panel of lawyers. And he has been making a tidy sum at the Home too."

Sujata was engaged in the daily care of her potted plants out in the balcony. She looked up, her eyes round with amazement, "What could his earnings be from the Home?"

Chhoton waved his mother off with a flick of his hand. "Is it possible to gauge everything from the outward appearance, Ma? Taking care of old women during their last days...many of those old hags out there have lots of money ..."

Jhinuk lost her temper at Chhoton's insinuation. "Do you know in what condition the residents of the Home live? How could you? You never visit Thamma! Have you ever seen how helpless they are? How pitifully they are left to their fate?"

"Oh stop it! Doesn't Thamma have enough money? Dadu's fixed deposit amounting to about a lakh, her widow's pension... Thamma has some jewellery too, doesn't she Ma? Perhaps that man squeezes money out of rich old widows. He might even hope that the old ladies will leave something for him in their wills."

Jhinuk had once spotted rows of coins under Charu Thamma's mattress. The old lady shared Mrinalini's room at the Home. The coins were kept for her grandson, who happened to be the only person who visited her. He came for those coins and quickly stole them while his grandmother pretended to look away. She would carefully arrange the coins every time she expected her grandson so that he continued to visit her.

How was Chhoton any different from that greedy, uneducated boy? The very thought left a bitter taste in Jhinuk's mouth.

She returned to her room and fingered those letters once more. The gloom from her mind disappeared every time she touched them. The pieces of paper and the few lines of writing, sinuously entangled her entire being. Yet, this bond did not demand anything of her. She was left free. It was an open, boundless space; a whole sky of freedom! A sky where Jhinuk could spread her golden wings like an eagle and skim through the air. She could fly higher. And higher.

Sharat had wondered whether Jhinuk would have enough patience to last her till the end. He was a fool. He didn't know that Jhinuk didn't have the power to stop herself and turn away. Not anymore.

~

Jhinuk lay resting in the afternoon the next day. Chhoton was out for a chat with his friends. Nilanjana suddenly entered her room and began firing a volley of questions at her. "What are your plans for this afternoon?"

Jhinuk sat up and stretched. "Nothing in particular. I might go to a play at the Academy with my colleague Madhuridi."

"I'm in big trouble. Have to meet Arunangshu today. I'm very nervous. Will you come with me?"

Jhinuk took some time to grasp the matter. Was Arunangshu the Boston guy? So he has landed in Calcutta after all? But why should Jhinuk go? What would she do there? Nilanjana's face was pink with embarrassment. "Please come along. I'm no good conversing. I'll feel confident if you are with me."

"You mean your families have finalised the wedding? Only the last hurdle remains?"

"There's no hurdle. The date has been fixed for the month of Sravan," Nilanjana winked, "Arunangshu wants a taste of formal courtship before the wedding. I ask you to come because it's the first day."

Jhinuk was amused. This was incredible – a wonderful mix of modernity and conservatism! She rolled her eyes and said, "Why should I be an unwanted third?"

Nilanjana still pleaded, "Please come with me. Arunangshu is very witty. You won't find him dull and boring."

Jhinuk didn't like hearing Nilanjana repeat Arunangshu's name so frequently. Nilanjana was such a brilliant student – did this piteous hankering after him become her?

"No, leave me out," Jhinuk yawned. "I've arranged the

programme with Madhuridi. She'll wait for me. Besides ..."

Meanwhile, Sujata had come in with two glasses of iced drinks. The tail end of the conversation had made her curious. "What's the matter?" she asked.

Jhinuk's eyes danced, "Marriage – in Sravan. After that, whoo-osh. Both will be off to the USA."

Sujata quickly blurted out, "Oh, Tunir's going next year too."

"Oh, Ma!" Jhinuk shook her head in exasperation, "His office has just started talking about it – and here you are, so sure he is going."

Sujata looked glum. "It's your habit to shrug off everything. Nilanjana dear, can't you give your friend a scolding? She's becoming more unmanageable every day!"

Nilanjana stared at both of them in bewilderment.

"Do you know what she did the other day? She went to the court to have a look at those ruffians! All alone, without breathing a word to anybody."

Jhinuk flared up, "Why should I go and tell anyone about it? You've gone and complained to the folks at mamarbari! You've mentioned it to Kakamoni. Have I committed a crime – a theft or a robbery?"

"Tell me Nilanjana, hasn't she demonstrated enough pluckiness? Her name was out in the papers, she was praised by everyone, what more? It's over now. Women shouldn't go beyond a certain point."

"What will she say? Does she have a mind of her own?" Jhinuk stepped in.

Nilanjana tried playing safe, "But your parents don't want you to ... the number of criminals is also on the rise ..."

Jhinuk glared at her friend, and didn't mince her words, "Nilu, this isn't your subject. Go home and meditate about Boston! That will help you in the future."

Jhinuk saw Nilanjana off and marched into Manas' room. Sujata followed her.

"Baba, tell me clearly what you folks want."

Manas had examination answer sheets piled high in front of him. He was engrossed in his work. He took off his glasses and looked up at his darling daughter, "What is it dear?"

"Don't you really want me to fight for a cause?"

"We certainly want you to!" replied Manas, absent-mindedly.

"Then why have all of you been dissuading me?"

Manas set his pile of papers aside. "Why are you losing your temper? We are parents. We worry. Shouldn't we think about your welfare and protection, about the dangers that might come your way?"

"Would you have stopped Chhoton, if it was him instead of me?"

"Yes, we would have," said Manas grimly. "Our fears for Chhoton would have been of a particular kind. But they are different from what we have for you. After all, you're a girl."

"You didn't say so all these years. Even when I was a child, you kept saying that a girl and a boy were the same. Why do you say different things now?"

Sujata snapped back before Manas did, "We let you study and

we let you work. But does that mean that you're man's equal?"

Jhinuk felt hot tears welling up her throat. Who said she wanted to be man's equal? Never! She wanted to be a human being.

A complete human being.

Chapter
Nine

*P*romita had come home for just twenty days this time. Mihir had some work in Bangkok and Singapore. He planned to spend a few days in Calcutta, after finishing his work and then returning to Montreal with wife and child. Mihir's parents' lived in Manicktala. It was a big house, a large family. Promita felt suffocated, staying there, during her short visit to India. She was far more at ease at her parents' house in Barasat, which lay beyond the outskirts of the city. She had spent only a few days at Manicktala, and had come to Barasat with Romita in tow.

With both their daughters staying with them after a span of eight long months, Dipti and Tapan had forgotten those dark days of anxiety and tension for a while. They were overjoyed and Tapan had decided to take leave from his office. The family had been out for a day's visit to the old temple towns of Nabadwip and

Mayapur, and had gone for a riverside picnic on the banks of the Ichhamati the next day.

Promita got transformed into a carefree young girl in her parents' home. There wasn't a single moment for the dark clouds of gloom to gather in Romita's mind. For the last couple of days, even the monsoon sky had smiled with bright sunshine, as though it was a part of the joyous mood prevailing in the house.

Tapan's tiny, single-storey house was tucked away in a cosy corner near Jessore Road. A bank officer, he had built it after taking a low-interest loan from his office. There was a small neat garden. Both Dipti and Tapan were keen gardeners, devoting their lonely days to that patch of green when their daughters had left home to marry. A wide variety of fresh vegetables and innumerable bright flowers made the place enchanting. A tall jackfruit tree stood near the eastern wall. The house didn't have too many rooms; a wide, circular balcony ran all along the southern part. This house was far more airy and well lit than the dark, stuffy, rented cubbyhole that was their old home in crowded Shyambazar.

Romita sat alone in the balcony, cleaning the fur of her favourite dog. It was a small milk-white, three-year old German Spitz. Romita had lovingly named it Bhaktaprasad. The dog had lost weight after Romita got married. He had become dirty too. It was difficult picking the fleas out from the thick fur. They had to be pinched out with the help of fingernails. But the insects would get lost in the white forest if one was slightly careless.

Promita wandered out of her room in a dishevelled state. She had a curly, fluffy mane of hair that reached her shoulders. Her nightgown was partly unbuttoned at the top. And her daughter Tuki was slung across her back. The tiny, one-year-old girl was a heavy child and one needed some amount of physical strength to carry her around.

Promita walked up to Romita and thumped down on the floor. "Why are you leaving today?" she asked. "Please stay for a few more days." Romita looked up at her sister. She was almost normal now: no dark circles round her eyes; her heart did not beat erratically at the slightest sound. She was more beautiful now, her old glowing charm back – she looked prettier than the mythical heavenly beauties, in her pale blue, lace nightgown. She patted Bhaktaprasad and said in mock grief, "Oh! I must go – there's important work at home."

"I'll give you a slap! How shameless you are!" Promita retorted in jest. "You've been away from Palash for just two days and you're already pining for him! Let me tell you Rumu, don't overdo things with husbands. They don't deserve it. They are a mighty dishonest lot!"

'Why? Is Mihirda secretly dating someone?"

"Rubbish! He doesn't even venture out to the seaside for fear of encountering flocks of bikini-clad women. Shows all his power over his poor wife. He doesn't even make the effort to get an ashtray for himself! He simply sits and yells, 'Mitu, get me the ashtray, will you!'" Suddenly, she hugged Romita, "My dearest darling sis," she cooed like old times, "Please don't go today." A suppressed anxiety rumbled inside Romita's heart. Palash would be collecting the report today, 'Dear God, let the suspicion turn out to be a false alarm!' For a moment Romita toyed with the idea of sharing her unease with her sister, then decided against it, and said, "I'm sorry, Didi. I simply have to leave today. I *do* have work at home."

Little Tuki stretched her hands out and pulled at Bhaktaprasad's soft fur. She toddled across to him and put her tiny palm into his mouth. The two sisters immediately switched their attention to her. Bhaktaprasad growled as soon as Romita pulled Tuki to herself. Promita squealed with laughter, "Goodness," she exclaimed, "How jealous he is!" Romita kissed Tuki on her chubby cheeks, "He's developing human habits living with us, what else?"

Promita was constantly preoccupied with charting out new plans. It didn't take her much time to switch from one topic to another. "You'll leave after tea, won't you? Let's go to a beauty parlour now. The super market has a new parlour, I believe? Let's get facials done. I need to trim my hair too."

"You mean here, in Barasat! Oh, what taste Didi! I won't ever get it done here."

"Hum-m-m! You've changed a lot in these eight months! Do you have to show off because you live in Ballygunge now? You were just a Shyambazar heroine ."

"It's not Ballygunge where I live now, it's Tollygunge. And I visit a beauty parlour in Bhowanipore. The place belongs to a friend of my mother-in-law. They do a good job with thermo herbs. I can take you there one day if you want. My mother-in-law and all my sisters-in-law are their regular customers."

"Isn't that too far? I believe there's a new market somewhere with shops from different Indian states. They have a wide choice of excellent saris ... last time Trishna took three exquisite saris back with her – two Bomkais and a Narayanpet." Romita stretched her legs on the polished green mosaic floor, with Tuki in her lap. She felt slightly sick after the breakfast of luchis that morning that lay heavy in her stomach. After a small burp she said, "Are you by any chance talking of Dakshinapan?"

"Yes, the name sounds that way. Isn't that in Bhowanipore?"

Romita was amused at her sister's ignorance. Her sister had travelled extensively across three continents with Mihirda, but she hardly knew Calcutta. Smiling, Romita said, "Not in Bhowanipore. It's Dhakuria."

Promita had already started planning, "How far is your mother-in-law's beauty parlour from there?" she asked.

"Not very far."

"Then let's go after lunch, we'll take a taxi first to your Dakshina Ban. I have to buy several nice saris."

Romita corrected her, "It's not 'ban.' It's 'pan.' Dakshin Apan, which literally means 'the shop in the south,' Dakshinapan."

"It's all the same." Promita took a quick decision, "Let's go. I can spend the night at Manicktala."

Romita hesitated, "But I'm supposed to go with Baba. What about that?"

"What will Baba do? He can't possibly sit outside the beauty parlour! He doesn't have to go. Won't you be able to get back to your husband's house alone from Bhowanipore?"

Promita could plan as fast as jet engine, she could take decisions as swiftly as a rocket shooting up in space, and she could travel all over the city with lightning speed. Barasat to Dhakuria, Dhakuria to Bhowanipore, Bhowanipore to Manicktala.

But Romita wasn't Promita. Perhaps she could have managed the same, two months earlier. But the question didn't arise now. Her relationship with Palash had improved, he wouldn't take offence if she went about alone. But what about his parents? Romita's heart beat faster. The nagging doubt pricked her mind once again. 'Dear God, don't let it be true! Please don't let it be true!'

Promita was extremely intelligent. She could anticipate her sister's dilemma at a glance. She assured her in a compassionate voice, "Don't worry. I'll drop you at your in-law's place and see you home safely."

The morning advanced. The dim monsoon sun of Sravan sent light signals through the jackfruit leaves. Tapan had left early – at the crack of dawn – with his fishing line and wheel. He had not yet returned. He had placed a bet last night with his daughters that he wouldn't return that morning without a catch for them. Tuki had left Romita and toddled back indoors, she came out again, holding her grandmother's hand. Dipti's worried eyes moved constantly to the gate.

Promita informed her mother, "I'm planning to go out with Rumu in the afternoon. I'll do some shopping, drop Rumu home and stay the night at Manicktala. Will you be able to manage Tuki alone for one night?"

Tuki gave little trouble. She had grown fond of her grandparents and would do fine staying away from her mother for just a night. Dipti was least worried about her. Other worries had left folds across her forehead. "Would it look right if you dropped Rumu home?"

"Oh, Ma! What's wrong with you? You've been behaving as though Rumu had been caught stealing!" Dipti looked at her elder daughter nervously. She was extremely fair, small-built and slim. Her large eyes were always full of apprehension.

Promita asked excitedly, "Tell me, what *is* the matter? What has happened that was so catastrophic? A few hooligans misbehaved with Rumu on the road. *They* committed the crime! They've been arrested too. And they will be punished. Over. Why must you break down in this manner?"

Dipti sighed, "This isn't your Canada or America, dear! This is India. Here, women suffer a lot."

"Rubbish! Women out there aren't better off either. Rapes and molestations take place by the dozen. The more advanced a country is, the worse the condition of women. Do you know that USA has ceremoniously installed rape clocks? The clocks are going to keep an account of the total number of rapes in the country. How disgusting!"

"Still, nobody bothers about these things in those countries, nor do they spread scandalous rumours about people."

"All countries are the same Ma. Raped women aren't exactly worshipped as idols even out there. The only difference is that women there are bolder and smarter so they protest a lot more. If the need arises, Rumu too will go to court, produce solid evidence and flatten their noses with a pumice stone! Rumu, won't you?" Romita's blood flowed faster. She could see Srobona Sarkar madly brandishing her heavy bag. Hitting hard.

Dark shadows gathered across Dipti's face. "If only her husband's family gave her the freedom! They are mighty proud of their family lineage! Haughty people, all of them!"

"But how do they come into the picture at all? This is entirely Rumu's problem," argued Promita. "Well, maybe Rumu's and Palash's problem. If his family behaves in too high and mighty a fashion, let him leave their house and set up his own place! He is an engineer, earns a tidy sum, the two of them will manage fine!"

Romita felt like laughing now. Palash talking back at his parents? Did Palash have the strength to control himself?

Tuki stood looking out of the grilled window, looking at Tapan coming through the gate. "Ta, ta, ta, ta" ... she squealed in delight. He held a huge fish in one hand; he clutched his line and wheel in the other. He was singing his favourite Rabindrasangeet in a loud hoarse voice, *"Tumi mor pao nai, pao nai parichay."* Promita ran up to her father and snatched the fish from his hands. She ran her fingers across the fish and cried with glee, "You've lost! You've lost the bet. It's a frozen fish!"

Tapan was tall and muscular. His features were sharp, like a Greek sculpture. He used to play football in his youth and had received calls at the state trial meets too. His job at the bank was also due to his being a good sportsman. His strong body shook with laughter, "You have caught me out! Is it cold – still? I told Dulal to dip the fish in water and defrost it properly!"

"You couldn't catch a fish even after sitting there so long?" Romita laughed like a musical clock. "I bet you sat on the banks of the pond, singing lustily to woo them to your hook."

"The fish are smarter these days. They don't want the standard bait! I suppose I'll have to give them noodles and pieces of kebab rolls next time. Ha, ha!"

Dipti went into the kitchen with the fish. Tapan threw his granddaughter up in the air and caught her back with his two hands. Tuki was overjoyed. She loved such rowdy games and continued to squeal, "Ta, ta, ta, ta..."

Tapan slumped down on a chair after a while and panted, "Wait child. I need to rest. What do you feed Tuktuki, Mitu? She's solid...!"

"The baby cereals are excellent in that country. And food is never adulterated."

"That's the reason why I tell Mihir, 'Don't talk of coming back.'"

"No Baba. Please don't encourage him. I'm eager to come back home."

Romita sat quietly next to her father. Even today, a strange sense of peace encompassed her when she sat next to him! She curled her lips. "It's common to experience sudden pangs of craving for the homeland if you stay abroad. Will you be able to come back and adjust once you're used to living out there? It's so horrible!"

"Whatever be the condition, I'm not staying back a day after Tuki turns ten. I can't imagine, my baby daughter dancing out of the house with her boyfriend every evening and I supplying her birth control pills! Impossible!"

Romita's eyes danced. "And suppose Mihirda doesn't want to come back?"

"He won't stay on without me!"

Mihirda was such a good husband! Romita's heart ached. Palash lost out to Mihirda completely, on all fronts!

Tapan's thoughts changed course as fast as Promita's. He agreed heartily, "That's right. Why should you live abroad? I'll start introducing the idea to Mihir when he visits us this time."

A moist wind blew outside. After a two-day respite, the monsoon clouds, fully armed, lined up in the sky. Promita pulled back her fluffy hair from her face and rolled it severely into a bun. "Why don't you make Baba some coffee?" she told her sister. "Bring me a cup too."

Promita snuggled up to her father as Romita left. She gave him a detailed description of the day's plan. Tapan leaned back on the chair and shrugged, "You plan to take Rumu back? I suppose you can. I can come with you, if you want."

"Baba, tell me, what's the matter? Ma said Palash doesn't want Rumu to appear in court as a witness?" Tapan threw open his hand expressing his helplessness.

"Can she afford to disregard the court's summons?" Promita demanded.

"If the court orders, the horse might walk up to the edge of the spring. But it's entirely up to the horse to decide whether he'll drink the water or not!" Tapan was used to speaking loudly. He quickly glanced indoors and lowered his voice as much as he could. "Palash claims he has been threatened by some people. He wants Rumu to appear in the court and declare that she can't recognize any of those boys. God knows whether this is true or not! I feel Palash is trying to dodge the court. That threat story is concocted. He doesn't want to proceed with the case, it's a question of prestige!"

"What kind of an explanation is this?" Promita was very annoyed. "Does Rumu know about it?"

"I don't think so. She hasn't told me anything."

"Strange! Isn't Rumu's honour Palash's honour too? Is Rumu worthless? If things are so bad, let her come over and stay here. She needn't live there any more. I'll see what they do then."

Tapan's voice turned thick. "She's a lot better since you came. I've seen her smiling and laughing after a long time. She was such a jolly girl – dressing up, going out shopping, buying new clothes and knick knacks ... in just a day the poor girl ..."

"I must say Rumu is overdoing things! Why does she bother? She should move around freely. You and Ma have mollycoddled her... she's too namby pamby! And look at Srobona Sarkar. She comes from a family like ours too!"

"If my blood had been younger, I could have dealt with those boys alone!" Tapan was about to raise his voice when he checked himself. "People have come to your Ma, melting with sympathy! But they didn't dare confront me! I had been thinking of going over to that Srobona girl's house. I stopped myself for Rumu's sake. Her husband's family doesn't want this ... Suppose she got into greater trouble?"

"Didn't Rumu get in touch with Srobona?"

Romita stood waiting at the door, with two mugs of steaming coffee in her hands. Her eyes were wide open. Her flushed face was completely drained of colour! Oh God, she was the centre of all the hushed discussions here too!

~

Romita felt dejected as usual as she left the parlour. Once again she couldn't bring herself to inspect that herbal 'look' of hers, created by plant juices. Was it her face? Or a mask? Well, it was definitely an impression of the contours of her face. How deftly they smeared her face with the herbal mix! And once it dried, the herbal mask was peeled off her skin, equally adroitly. Every speck of dirt from the pores of her skin stuck to the mask. The face turned brighter, clearer, and smoother. Romita sighed softly. If only life was like that! The skilful hands of a sorcerer could then peel off the dry, shrivelled layer of stigma from her body! And life would be back in deeper, brighter shades!

Promita talked nineteen to the dozen with her sister's mother-in-law's friend. The lady was delighted to have served a customer from Canada. Her aging face was carefully toned and made-up – amorous shades played on the deftly hidden wrinkles. Her neatly plucked eyebrows and thickly outlined eyes were bashful. Her bobbed hair bounced back and forth as she said coyly, "Do come again."

The two sisters had a good laugh at the woman's affected

voice and gestures. People on the road turned to look at them but Promita didn't care. She had shopped to her heart's content. Quite a few saris and dress material. Bric-a-brac for home décor. An expensive Pochampalli sari for her sister. Silk- cotton saris for her mother and mother-in-law. She bent both ways alternately, weighed down by the heavy plastic bags. Almost like the seasaw in a children's park!

There had been a few spells of heavy downpour since the afternoon. Even now, tiny droplets of water moved like fine pollen grains and moistened the air. The wet tar on the road caught the glow of light from street lamps and sparkled like diamond chips. The evening had deepened.

Even after a long day and a good deal of travelling, Promita wasn't tired. She came to the crossing of Hajra Road and suggested, "Let's take the Metro. The Calcutta Metro is so good ..."

Romita vigorously shook her head, "No, no! Let's take a cab." The taxi driver couldn't dictate his terms and bargain with Promita. She would go both south and north!

Promita talked incessantly once inside the taxi, her words gushed out like a mountain spring. Her husband was so absent-minded and ...he never bought anything for his wife, not even a bottle of perfume, let alone bigger gifts. Her parents-in-law unreasonably insisted on making another trip to Canada. Promita had wanted to take her own parents this time. How her sisters-in-law managed to take all the cosmetics she had brought as gifts, as soon as she landed in Calcutta! They had been to Alaska for a holiday before coming home. It was bitterly cold! A snow desert! Mihir wanted to teach Tuki swimming early. Promita disagreed. Etcetera. Etcetera. Strings of words, rising like an exuberant waterfall, fell on Romita's ears and scattered in all directions. Except for a few nods and a couple of 'Hums', Romita was silent. How happy Didi was! How lucky!

The taxi was hopelessly stuck at the Rashbehari crossing for a while. A traffic jam! Promita's restless eyes ran out of the cab's window. "Oof, there's been such a population explosion in Calcutta!" she exclaimed.

Romita looked out of the window. Who was that walking along the pavement on the right? Wasn't that Srobona Sarkar? In a deep blue kameez with white polka dots. White salwar. White dupatta. Yes, it was Srobona alright! There was a tall man with her. They walked, talking intimately to each other. They walked towards Romita's taxi. Did Srobona's eyes touch Romita's momentarily while the two of them crossed the road? Romita's heart yearned to shout across to her, "Srobonadi, here I am. This way. Srobonade..e..e." No sound escaped her voice, her throat was dry. And her pulse rate shot up abnormally.

Srobona got lost in the human jungle.

Romita leaned back against the taxi seat. She panted without reason. Promita didn't notice the change in her sister. As the throng cleared and the taxi started moving, she too, leaned back. "At last. Thank God!" she exclaimed.

Golf Club Avenue came nearer. Promita said, "It's quite late now, nearly eight. I'm not getting down." Romita glanced at her sister, relieved. She didn't actually want Promita to come upstairs. She wasn't sure what the reception would be like; how her in-laws would take to the idea of her sister dropping her home so late at night. Still, she formally invited her sister to come with her. "Drop in for a little while. Just show your face, say hello and leave."

Promita hesitated. "Will you be in trouble if I don't?"

"No, I don't mean that! They aren't bad people." Romita felt slightly embarrassed, "I'm sure my mother-in-law will be glad to see you."

"Not today. I'll drop in one day before I finally leave. Definitely. That's a promise! Please explain ... to them."

The taxi backed out after dropping Romita. She climbed up to the first floor with the sari packet in her hand. Her knees seemed to suddenly give in. The anxiety building up within her over the past few days began churning in her mind once again. Romita touched the coral on her finger for support, 'Dear God! Let the suspicion be false.'

Palash was watching television with his mother. The house seemed quite empty. Leena and Ashok were probably out. Hearing Romita's footsteps, both of them turned to look. Romita came up to her mother-in-law. "Didi dropped me home. Have a look at this sari, isn't it pretty? Didi bought it for me."

Her mother-in-law unpacked the sari from its cardboard box and turned it over to examine it. The soft pink background had chocolate brown motifs embroidered on it. "Beautiful! How much?"

"Fourteen hundred – twelve hundred after a discount."

"It's extremely pretty. Why didn't your sister come up?"

"She had to go back to Manicktala. She'll come another day."

"You could have spent a few more days at your parents' place. Your sister has come a long way to see you," Romita's mother-in-law smiled benevolently.

Romita's eyes met Palash's. She quickly searched for an answer to her nagging doubt in his eyes. She couldn't find one.

Star TV showed the glamourous lifestyle of famous Hollywood film stars. Romita's mother-in-law's eyes soon went back to this wonderful world of wealth and luxury. Romita stared at the screen for a few seconds and went in. Palash followed her to the bedroom. Before Romita could ask him questions, he picked her up in the air and spun her around twice. The two bodies rolled into the bed. Romita freed herself somehow. "What's the matter with you! The door is ajar, Ma is sitting outside!" Palash jumped up quickly, shut the bedroom door and came back to the bed. "Oof!" he exclaimed. "You had made me nervous. I had been waiting so long for you. If you hadn't come back tonight, I would have spent the night out in the balcony."

Romita turned sideways to face Palash. Drim drim drim drim – her heart thumped, louder with every passing moment.

"Did you collect the report?"

"What do you think?" Palash lovingly played with Romita's slim white fingers – as delicate and pretty as the half-blooming buds of rajanigandha. "I did darling. I did!"

Drim drim drim drim drim drim drim drim – the heart drummed harder! "Well, what does the report say?"

Palash looked deeply into Romita's eyes, "Haven't you got the answer already dear?"

Romita's body went limp. Palash held her in his arms and flooded her with passionate kisses and caresses, "What shall it be, my darling?" he cooed. "A boy? Or a girl?"

The suspicion had turned out to be true after all! Oh God!

"Anybody is welcome," Palash went on jovially, "But I would prefer a girl."

Romita closed her eyes, trying to accept her fate. Palash thought Romita was enjoying his caress. "Darling? Why aren't you speaking? What is it you want?" he continued asking.

Would a girl be another Romita? Or would she be a Srobona Sarkar? Romita parted her lips slightly and managed to say, "A boy would be better."

"Eh, you like boys, don't you?"

"Not bad! He'll be a naughty and a spirited little boy. Rowdy and restless!"

"You love rowdies, don't you?" Palash smiled cheekily.

Romita froze for a moment. Realising that he shouldn't have said that, Palash kissed his wife lightly on the lips to ease her tension. "Don't you understand I was pulling your leg? Girls and boys are quite the same these days. And if you're really keen, you can always get a test done. You'll know whether it's a son or a daughter."

Romita's eyes moved across to the window. She wanted to clear other doubts as well. She asked in a shaky, listless voice, "Has the doctor given the date?"

Palash let go of Romita and stood up,"He said this was the eighth week."

Romita thought to herself, "I know. I knew!"

"He must have given the date it is expected – what is it?" Palash fished out a bunch of papers from his bag and hunted for the prescription. Romita's mind had begun to flow backwards, against the current of time. Her calculations were correct! Eighth week. That meant seven to ten days after the Tollygunge incident!

Palash looked at the piece of paper and kept it on the table. "End of February," he declared. "Twenty seventh."

Romita didn't hear him speak. It was just a single day during that period. Just one single day that…! The memories of that night, of absolute humiliation and indignity, shook her mind and body with a sudden, new frenzy. Romita's eyes floated out of the window once again to the distant horizon. During these moments, when she lay deeply absorbed in thought, her beauty transcended to ethereal heights! She got transformed into an unknown bird of paradise, and was no longer an ordinary earth woman. She couldn't be touched then, only gazed at. As if a touch would melt her away like a dream and Palash would never be able to find her.

Palash leaned towards her slowly, almost hypnotized. "What are you thinking about, darling?" he asked. "Can you hear me?

Thinking of the one who is arriving? About the child born out of our love?"

A cord snapped somewhere deep inside Romita's heart. Did love exist that night? The child was the fruit of a purely biological urge – with a total disregard for Romita's likes and dislikes. How cruel are the laws of nature!

Chapter
Ten

*J*hinuk stopped midway before entering the headmistresses' room. A burly man of about thirty-five with closely cropped hair sat inside.

Sunita called her inside, "Come in. Do you know this gentleman? He happens to be your pupil, Yudhajit's, father. He has a complaint."

Jhinuk was ravenously hungry. She hadn't had time for a proper meal before leaving for school that morning. She had got late because of a long conversation with her parents. A mysterious telephone call had been coming to their house at the stroke of midnight for the last three days. Her father had answered the call twice and her mother once. The call would get disconnected on the other end as soon as someone answered it. Initially, Jhinuk didn't pay much heed to them. It was only after noticing how anxious her parents were, that she had suggested reporting the incident to the local police station. But her parents became even more distraught.

"What happened in your class yesterday?" Sunita asked her.

What had happened – Jhinuk couldn't recollect immediately. Anxiety overlaid her sharp pangs of hunger like a thin coat of sweat. She couldn't think clearly. "Is it true that you flogged some children in your class during the last period yesterday? Especially this gentleman's son ..."

"I never say that madam." The grumpy man moved uneasily in his chair. "I say she told my son something nasty and now the child is terrored. He don't want to attendance school."

Trying her best to stop herself from laughing aloud at the man's awful grammar, Jhinuk suddenly recollected yesterday's incident. Two boys had been fighting during the last period, using their wooden rulers as swords. As soon as Jhinuk had snatched the rulers away and had begun to check the children's classwork, the two snarling boys had flung themselves at each other, like a tiger fighting a wild boar. They fought with empty hands, charging at each other, scratching and biting with all their might. Children normally turned very restless during the last period; they had to be strictly controlled. Jhinuk had simply boxed the boys' ears – and this had brought one of the fathers running to the school to complain! And Sunita had actually hauled up Jhinuk to demand an explanation right there – in front of the boy's guardian!

"Children should be punished when they are naughty. But they mustn't skip school because of it. That's not right!" Jhinuk answered back defiantly.

The man didn't look at Jhinuk, he spoke to Sunita instead, "My son say that she warning him, 'You're becoming a hooligan! But mind you, I know very well controlling hooligans!'" The man's tone was brash and impolite, making Jhinuk's blood boil. "Yes, I did," she said. "So what?" The man continued to address Sunita, "There are other aunties who scold children also. But you see me interference with that? The kids are very scared of the lady these days, after the Tollygunge Metro station incident." Jhinuk didn't know whether to laugh or to cry.

"Right," Sunita said to the gentleman, matter of factly. "We've heard what you had to say. Send your boy to school from tomorrow. I don't think there will be any further problem."

"Well, good if there is no. Goodbye. The neighbourhood boys have made garden in the park with rabbits and guinea pigs. I have to kick it off." The man got up from his chair, "It's hurt my son's prestige. He can't tolerance people terroring him."

Jhinuk's face was red with suppressed anger. Sunita toyed with the paperweight. "You heard the guardian's complaint?"

"You ... you ... you entertained that silly complaint? That uneducated, ill-mannered ...!"

"Mind your language, Srobona. Here in this school, all guardians are to be treated as equals. Guardians are guardians. I don't differentiate between a gentleman and a boor. By the way, do you know who he is? He happens to be a councillor of the municipality. His services might come in handy when the need arises." Sunita glanced at the desk calendar. "Let's forget about the complaint. However, I must say that of late your attitude and manner of speaking have undergone a change. You were never so harsh before or so aggressive!"

"I – aggressive!"

"Well, what I mean by aggressive is that you lack softness in your character. Do you know why women are preferred as teachers of little children? It is to ensure that they grow up within a circle of care and affection. The children expect to see a mother-figure in their teacher – I mean they want someone gentle and affectionate."

But Jhinuk was still the same Jhinuk. She hadn't become someone else. So where was the need to remind her to be gentle with children?

Sunita shook her head, "Mr Sengupta was saying the other day that handling children is an extremely difficult and delicate job."

Demonic hunger was raging inside her head. But Jhinuk kept her cool as far as possible, "I see you've already discussed the matter with Mr Sengupta!"

Sunita didn't seem to mind the subtle hint of sarcasm. "No, I haven't yet spoken to him about this, of course," she said quickly. "He was only making very general comments. One has to handle the children of the present generation with a lot more caution and tact. The school is going to felicitate you on August 15. He plans to speak on the subject on the same day and give a guideline to teachers on handling children."

Jhinuk's head was still hot and throbbing with suppressed anger when she returned to the staff room, hunger still ravaging her belly. She opened her tiffin box, took out a sandwich and munched away with vengeance. Hitting the hard-boiled egg against a wooden table and breaking open its shell, she glared angrily at the egg after taking a mouthful. It was poultry stuff, with its disgustingly colourless, pale yellow yolk. Gobindo's Ma knew very well that she hated poultry eggs, yet ... She spat a mouthful of egg out of the window behind her and returned resentfully to the soggy slice of bread-and-butter.

There was a heated discussions going on at the other end of the room. Madhuri was on leave for a few days. Gitali spotted Jhinuk and came near her. "Why do you look so disprited? What did that man come for?" she asked.

"That councillor!" Jhinuk was about to raise her voice when Gitali warned her with her eyes, "Softly," she said. "The furniture in this room have eyes and ears." That was true to an extent. Sunita's secret spies were always on the alert picking up every relevant bit of conversation. Jhinuk emptied a full glass of water.

Gitali brought her mouth close to Jhinuk's ears. "Before the man became a councillor, he was the local thug. He went up the social ladder and got himself elected to the local civic body, graduating to a Mr Banerjee from his nickname Khatash. His men still go round extracting money forcibly from the owners of shops and markets." The reason for Sunita summoning Jhinuk to her room for an explanation became clearer. The man didn't serve the school in any way. All that talk of the man being a help to the school was a cock and bull story. It was simply fear. She had to run the school after all.

Gitali heaved a sigh of relief after listening to the details from Jhinuk. "Thank god," she said, "there wasn't much trouble. But let me tell you something Srobona, you've become quite reckless lately – the 'don't care' type. You're talking too much and too sharply, using words that are too strong for people's liking."

Jhinuk quickly tore open a bubblegum. "Why do you say that, aunty? What have I done?"

"Well, if I remember correctly, you misbehaved with another guardian just a few days back. Sunitadi doesn't know about it. I didn't tell her."

Jhinuk rubbed her toe on the floor stubbornly. "I didn't misbehave. A hundred-rupee note was found in the child's pocket so I summoned the mother to warn her about it."

"I know."

"Well, you don't know the entire story, aunty. Surprisingly enough, the lady was very rude to me. She told me, 'Is it your business to check whether my son has five rupees or five hundred rupees in his pocket?' I was forced to remind her that this was a school, and not a place to flaunt wealth. 'Kindly don't stuff your son's pockets with money, before sending him to school everyday' I had said ! This is part of our school's decorum. Was I wrong aunty? Did I make a mistake?"

"I never said you were wrong!" Gitali sounded exasperated. "The lady complained to me too. She was extremely hurt. Your attitude and your way of talking were not very polite. I've known you since you were a child. And I'm still watching you. Lately, there's far too much logic—too strong for people's liking—in whatever you say and do. In fact, you're going overboard with it. You have acquired a tendency to enter into heated arguments. Maybe, I haven't been able to explain the problem clearly enough, Srobona. Well, it's like this ... you're somewhat brusque ... a little too manly, perhaps, in your behaviour." Jhinuk was taken aback by this sudden attack. She couldn't figure out where it hit her most. A million shards of glass had entered her blood stream; they circled her entire being, contaminating her heart and lungs.

The sky had been like a filthy dustbin – a particularly dirty shade of grey – since morning. Jhinuk walked home slowly from the tram depot. To her right were the film studios; a large crowd had gathered at the gate. Someone had died. The body was placed on a lorry. A young film actress was busy garlanding the corpse, her eyes carefully hidden behind huge sunglasses. People jostled with each other, craning their necks to snatch a glimpse of the silver screen heroine. There wasn't a trace of curiosity anywhere about the dead man.

On other days, Jhinuk stopped for a while at the groundfloor landing before climbing up the stairs. She would open the family letterbox and make a routine check of the mail. Today, she was completely disinterested. Even on reaching their own flat, she had a quick, quiet lunch, went to her room and lay down on her bed.

Sujata had noticed her daughter's glum face. "What's wrong dear?"

"Nothing, just feeling out of sorts."

"Nilanjana had come in the morning. She came to invite you."

Sujata picked up the wedding card smeared with turmeric paste and handed it to Jhinuk.

Jhinuk unfolded the card and glanced through it. Twenty eighth of Sravan. That was August 13. The Friday after the next. There was a separate note inside the envelope – a special invitation for Tunir.

"Did you go to the police station after all?"

Jhinuk was looking at the pretty card, decoratively shaped like a palanquin. Her mother's query hadn't entered her head. She asked absent-mindedly, "Why the police station?"

"Didn't you say this morning, that you might drop in at the thana to report the strange phone calls?"

"Oh, should I rush to the thana just because I happened to mention it once? As if I have no other work to do. Silly calls... could be a wrong connection or simply a mechanical fault with the telephone itself... you never know! If you're so nervous about it, you should take off the receiver when you go to bed every night!"

It was not clear whether Sujata was pacified by this solution – she muttered to herself, "Fair enough. Good sense has finally prevailed. At least you didn't run to the thana this time. You've turned so haughty and brazen lately ... putting men to shame! Rushing down to the thana whenever you feel like it ... standing face to face with ruffians and criminals at the court! Is there a fragment of womanliness left in you?"

The words chugged out like a long trail of innumerable railway luggage vans. The air churned by the fan in this closed room had turned uncomfortably warm. Jhinuk clenched her teeth. She didn't wish to counter her mother's words. But they continued to sting: "Srobona, you're turning too manly. Srobona, you're brash. Srobona, you're aggressive. Outdoing men by your belligerence. You don't have a trace of womanliness in you."

Heaviness descended like an avalanche in Jhinuk's heart.

For her, the days dragged on heavily. The first day. The second. Third. The daily routine continued. She went to school as usual. Came home. And the rest of the time, she stayed in resolutely. She examined herself a million times in front of the dressing table mirror, the bathroom mirror, even the rusty, spotted mirror in the school toilet. Thoroughly. Going over every inch of her body in great detail. Had she really changed? The state of the mind is always reflected on one's looks. But her physical charm was intact. In that case, did the transformation lie deeper in subtler layers of the mind? What did people mean by the word 'manly'? And what did 'womanliness' imply? Lack of confidence? An unquestioning loyalty? Or did Jhinuk remain the same person as before? It was just a single unusual act that had torn her asunder from the circle of her commonplace life.

Tunir hadn't shown himself for the past few days. Jhinuk had called him at his office. But Tunir seemed to be horribly busy. The company's chairman Mr Jones was visiting from California. Tunir would probably even refuse to see Death if he came calling at the moment. This was a rat race! In these desperate times even a second's distraction...a moment's shaky recoil in his thigh muscles would send him reeling off the track.

Jhinuk recovered herself somewhat after Chhoton came visiting in the weekend. Chhoton continued to pull her leg, crack jokes, stretch his palm out to Didi for money, whenever he got the opportunity. He had been recently introduced to cigarettes and Didi was his main financial support, providing the money for his new addiction. Jhinuk would shout at him, be angry, but she would still give him the money. And happily too.

Jhinuk set off after lunch on Sunday for Bishakha's house. They would have to buy a gift for Nilanjana. Jhinuk and her friends had given Bishakha the responsibility of buying gifts and collecting contributions for the group since their days at college. Jhinuk would be free of all responsibility after she paid her share of the common fund for the wedding gift.

It was a lovely day. The sun rested behind a flimsy cover of clouds. A light wind swished about. It wasn't hot.

Bishakha's tiny room had piles of books and papers scattered all over. Bishakha lay sprawled across the pile, drowned in her tape recorder. She was listening to some awful cassette with great concentration. Jhinuk was about to speak, when Bishakha signalled with her eyes, asking her not to talk but quietly sit down.

Jhinuk tried listening to the cassette for a few seconds. A dry discussion in English on prawns, environmental pollution and weather! Jhinuk switched off the tape.

"Ishh. You have muddled up everything. I have to start right from the beginning all over again."

Jhinuk pouted her lips, "Are you determined to bore me to death?"

Bishakha rolled over on the floor in her oversize kaftan, "This is a job in transcription. Oof, it's boring!"

"What on earth were those people talking about?"

"That was a group discussion on prawn cultivation."

"Since when have you been interested in prawn cultivation?"

"Not prawns. I'm interested in cash. Money. Sweet money. It's a part-time job. Whatever I manage to get out of it, is good enough. Last week, I worked on truck tyres. Tell me what's a tyre's guti?"

Jhinuk didn't seem the least excited.

"You see, they pay fairly well. Two hundred rupees per topic. The job is simply data compilation. Mainak is also at it."

"Any news about Mainak's job?"

"Nothing. He's eking out a living by doing odd jobs like this one. He wrote a newspaper feature last week. I think he's got himself another assignment in a weekly magazine."

"You two had better come to a decision, a settlement of some sort. Mashima is suffering from acute tension."

"Wait. Let him find ground under his feet."

"You've got a job. Won't you two be able to manage with that?"

"Well, I might be able to scratch out a living of some kind." Bishakha ran her fingers lightly through the silky strands of her shampooed hair. "But how would I keep Mainak's ego under control? He might mouth big slogans on social progress and women's liberation but would he accept the situation and agree to live on his wife's earnings?"

Bishakha collected the scattered papers and put them away in a bunch. She had taken out the cassette from the tape recorder and kept it on the side of the bed.

Jhinuk fished out some money from her bag, "What have you planned to buy for Nilanjana?"

"A musical clock. She'll be reminded of us every hour as the clock chimes." Bishakha put the money away. "What have you told Nilu? She seemed very upset with you and said the most terrible things."

"Oh, she always does. What new crime have I committed?"

"She wanted to take you to Mr. Boston, but you refused. True?"

"It's true. But that happened long ago. Nilu still remembers that?"

"Nilanjana Ghosh doesn't ever forget anything. She says she promised Boston that she would show him a friend who was different, not a bit like herself, who could fight criminals if necessary. Brave and spirited – A fighter. Someone whose pictures are published in the papers."

"So?"

"Well, her fighter friend didn't turn up – quite a damper for her prestige."

"Hey, why do you keep calling me fighter?"

"Come on, didn't you get into a brawl?"

"I protested against ruffians creating a public nuisance. Is that the same as getting into regular street fights?"

"Wow! What logic boss!" Bishakha burst into laughter. She glanced at Jhinuk and covered her face with her hand in mock fear. "Srobona, please don't look at me like that. You make my heart tremble!"

Jhinuk didn't smile. She stared at Bishakha unblinkingly. A friend indeed!

"You don't know boss, there's a macho streak developing in you," Bishakha sniffed the air hard. "Hum...m...m. I think I can smell male arrogance. Musty? Hot and spicy!"

The air was heavy with sudden pathos, as if someone had pulled the string of violin. Jhinuk picked up a women's magazine lying on the cane stool and flipped through the pages. The grey, cloudy sky outside entered her mind afresh. The mood of monsoon months swept into the room.

Bishakha hardly paid attention to Jhinuk. "I shall be getting another topic shortly. Will you join me? We can work together. You'll like the subject." She rambled on.

Jhinuk's eyes were stuck to a picture in the magazine. It wasn't exactly a picture but the design of a knitted pullover for men. A combination of navy blue, maroon and mustard yellow. It would look perfect on Tunir's slim body. She could almost smell Tunir inside that pullover. What was he doing at this moment while thick clouds hung heavy in the sky? Keeping her eyes fixed on the picture, Jhinuk asked, "What's the topic?"

"Harrassment of working women in public transports. Isn't it interesting?"

"Yeah, good enough. Not bad." Jhinuk put the magazine back in its place.

"Are you coming with me?"

"No."

Jhinuk stuck her bubblegum against her palate.

"You have just arrived! Must you leave now? Are you going to see Tunir?"

Jhinuk quickly gulped the breath which stuck in her throat. Tunir was now looking for a ladder to rise in the world. Well, let him! The earth was gradually turning friendless for Jhinuk. She was lonely. Where would Jhinuk head for, now?

Chapter
Eleven

*J*hinuk felt a bit relaxed as she neared Shantiparabar. It was an old-style double-storeyed building, with a boundary wall around it. There was a small plot of land next to the gate. The huge mango tree that grew beside the wall was fruitless, with a thick foliage – so thick that it almost completely guarded the home from the bustling world beyond. Traffic flowed in a continuous stream down the main road, from morning till late at night. There were no sights just sounds. An invisible world of sounds was the only link between the stagnant life within the house and the bustling world outside.

Mrinalini was sitting out in the first floor balcony, like she did every evening. Bewildered, her face rife with anxiety, she watched Jhinuk approaching. She blurted out, "Oh, how is it that you're here today? I hope things are fine at home? How is everybody? Rumki? Your aunts?"

"Good heavens! Everybody's fine!" Jhinuk raised her hands to reassure her. "Your daughter had been swimming in the flood waters of Alipurduar for some days, but she's fine now. Babua is just back after a thorough investigation. He is coming over to our house today to spend the night with Chhoton. They've fixed a whole-night video programme for themselves. Endless session of song-and-dance on the screen! And ilishmaachh."

Mrinalini's fair, wrinkled face broke into a smile. It was a fixed, wooden smile that seemed not to come from the heart. Her lips were slightly parted as a concession to 'happiness.' Her sons and daughters-in-law seldom visited her; Chhoton, Babua never did. She had seen Chhoton just once last month. But Babua hadn't visited her in a long time. Her vision was weakening day by day. And she feared that one day soon, she wouldn't be able to recognise them even if she saw them!

A cluster of old women sat hunched in the west balcony – quiet, without budging. Pale rays of fading sunlight lay huddled at their feet. Jhinuk looked at one of the chairs and smiled cheerfully. "Is your knee any better?"

Signs of life were visible in the chair. "No dear. Natu's son didn't turn up this week too!"

"You won't be able to communicate from this distance, madam. Prabha-Ma's hearing has gone. There's no dial tone. The receiver is dead."

Startled by an unexpected male voice, Jhinuk looked back. It was Sharat! Did he come, like autumn, breaking through the rain clouds? Or, did he sprout from under the earth like one of those fairy-tale characters in children's books?

"You – on a Sunday? It's not your day today."

Sharat Ghoshal looked doubly amazed, "*You* on a Sunday? That's not *your* day either."

They laughed aloud together. The wave of rippling laughter caused the chairs to stir and shift positions for a brief second. Soon enough, they were back to their habitual immobility.

Mrinalini beckoned Jhinuk to sit out in the balcony and left for some errand in her room. Jhinuk sat talking to Sharat. Her acquaintance with Sharat Ghoshal had grown closer during the past two months. Sharat had spent the time painstakingly explaining the intricacies of law to her. And Jhinuk had come to know a good deal about Sharat too. He had been a schoolmaster before he took up this job at the court. He lived alone in Usthi, near Ramrampur. He had picked up homeopathy from books. Didn't have much interest in the court job. But battled it out with those cases he liked.

"What about the ashram you had planned to establish? How far has the work progressed?" asked Jhinuk.

"My goodness!" Sharat exclaimed. "My plan has become public!"

"You're in the same boat as these old grannies you've been visiting so long! Suffering from loss of memory!" Jhinuk smiled at him. "You told me about it yourself, while you sat on that particular chair about twelve days ago."

"Did I? That means your name is down there too."

"Where?"

"In the list of donors. I had been talking to Mrinal-Ma about this. I shall have to ask for a donation from anyone I discuss my plans with."

Jhinuk frowned.

Sharat continued to explain, gesticulating with his hands. "There's this tiny plot of land. But a patch of land won't help to build a whole ashram! There should be thatched hutments at least, for the inmates. I don't have to build brick and cement buildings in the village. The kind of people who will stay there are totally unaccustomed to cement houses. They will probably spend sleepless nights in them!"

"How much is Thamma donating?"

Sharat was quick to catch the discordant note in Jhinuk's question and responded accordingly. "Are you thinking of donation only as money? And why would people donate money? How can I ask for it? That would be an outrageous audacity on my part! I would request you to donate a wee bit of physical labour, that's all. A little support for women who have been thrown out of their homes; love and care for a few orphan children; giving them proper education…not just knowledge lifted out of text books but the kind that would help them develop a clear vision of the world around them. Teaching a little needlework to the women, for instance, trying to make them forget that they have nobody to care for them in this world, what else!"

Mrinalini came and settled down in a chair. She muttered to

herself, "He's planning to blow away whatever little money he has made."

"Don't you pay heed to what Mrinal-Ma says. She has decided to go and stay there herself. She plans to teach handicrafts to the women."

"Thamma will leave Shantiparabar and go away! Oh, no!"

Mrinalini declared dispassionately, "I have spent quite a few days anchored at this harbour! If you ask me, it's getting too crowded for my liking! Haven't you seen the waiting list of applicants on the notice-board? The present inmates of this place were down in a waiting list themselves! And now you have a second waiting list of those who want to come and stay! Isn't that funny?"

"I don't find it funny at all," Jhinuk replied dryly. "Why must you go away?"

"Crazy child! Am I leaving this moment? I just plan to anchor my boat at a different port for the final leg of the journey, that's all."

Jhinuk's face fell. What on earth was the matter with Thamma! Why did she have to – at her age – tag along with this crazy middle-aged fellow and his uncertain ways, move to some distant out-of-the-way village and spend the rest of her life there! But if Thamma has made up her mind, she would definitely go. Jhinuk was sure of that.

"You look pretty upset!" Sharat exclaimed. "It is still at the planning stage. We have a long way to go. Better think of your pending case instead. Time for that has arrived. I heard they've engaged an even more well known lawyer."

"They had a good lawyer last time too!"

"Oh, he'll be there alright. He's a small fry compared to the person who is coming now. After all, the case happens to involve big shots and influential families! Robinda told me, the other day, that the doctor was nominated for the sheriff's post about three years ago."

"Well, maybe he was. I'm not sure. You can't expect me to keep track of everything!"

"But you must! How will you prepare yourself for the fight if you don't have a clue about your enemy's powers!"

"Oh, I'm ok. I just hope Romita Choudhury doesn't mess it all up! If she cooperates, even the best lawyer from the Supreme Court won't be able to stop them from sailing into jail!"

Sharat laughed indulgently, as elders do, at a child's bravado, spinning a story of an imaginary tiger hunt. "Good!" he said, in an encouraging tone. "Confidence wins half the war. According to my calculations, even if Romita Choudhury goes back on her words, your personal account as witness to the crime might lead to their punishment. It may not be a severe one, but definitely adequate. However, you have to keep certain things in mind. Too much self-confidence loses the war. The jungle might be silent but it's never empty! The tiger might be asleep, or planning its hunt. You shouldn't forget that they have sharp claws and teeth honed to perfection. By the way, did you know something? That particularly helpful O.C. has been transferred in the interest of public service!"

"What do you mean? He had got posted only in March!"

"Don't you understand? He arrested those Romeos promptly after the crime, sent a no-nonsense report to the court, kept the boys in the lock-up for a fortnight – doesn't he have to pay for his actions? This is pretty common among the police."

Suddenly, Jhinuk debated whether to tell Sharat about the ghost calls she had received. She decided otherwise. Sharat Ghoshal might think she was nervous. After a moment's silence, she asked, "What happened to that woman with the two kids – the one who had gone to ask for her alimony and was beaten up by the husband? The court was supposed to give a verdict soon."

"Oh, don't mention it. That was a horrible mess! The judgement was out the day before yesterday. The fellow got a year's imprisonment."

"Oh, that's jolly good news indeed!"

"My reaction was the same when I heard it." Sharat grinned, "But as soon as we were out of the magistrate's room, that woman started abusing me. Never mind, if her husband didn't give her alimony or look after the children! That didn't matter at all to her – instead, she accused *me* of sending her husband to jail. Kicked up a fuss because I made her husband suffer!"

For quite some time, the sound of raised voices floated from below – the noise seemed to have increased suddenly. Sharat walked up to the railing to see.

"That's Anu's voice," Mrinalini concluded. "She screams a lot. Somebody told her that the downstairs office stole all the letters from her family, so they never reached her. She had lost all count of days and months already; now she has lost all sense of time as well. She doesn't seem to remember that the post office is closed today ..."

Sharat turned back and looked at her. "Tell me Mrinal-Ma, do Sundays, Mondays, Tuesdays – days and nights have any particular relevance in this house?"

"They certainly do," Mrinalini smiled. "Don't you see how empty the entire first floor is on a Sunday evening? The whole lot is downstairs, watching TV in the office room. They even devour the commercials!"

Sharat's deep, dark eyes twinkled. "Well, you must admit Mrinal-Ma, that the TV commercials are pretty exciting stuff! Don't they remind you of the past, bring you a whiff of excitement. I'd better leave now. Goodbye. I'll just peep into Sushila-Ma's room and go straight home." Sharat hurried out.

The evening had died out. Jhinuk's eyes remained fixed on the mango tree outside for a long time. Homebound birds chirped joyfully around its bare, fruitless branches. Jhinuk listened to the sound, all ears. Suddenly, she clutched Mrinalini's hand. "Don't you ever feel lonely Thamma?"

Mrinalini held on to Jhinuk's hand and rose from the chair. "Come in," she said.

There were three beds. Three small wooden stools. A small cupboard next to each bed. Trunks piled high against the cupboards. Wooden racks with mirrors fixed to grooves in the wall. Strings stretched across the room for hanging clothes. There were shelves for placing the clay images of numerous gods. The freshly whitewashed walls were a forest of nails and hooks. Pictures of the children and grandchildren of the three inmates hung from this forest – their husbands too. Movement was difficult in a room which was packed with things.

Lighting incense sticks, Mrinalini squatted in front of her gods. She always sat down to a few minutes of meditation after sundown. Jhinuk knew Thamma didn't have much faith in God. Yet, why did she observe the daily ritual of meditation! Perhaps it was a process of coming to terms with herself – the clay images were a mere excuse!

Jhinuk looked at the pictures on the wall. Most of them had faded a great deal. There was a big group photograph on Mrinalini's portion of the wall. Only she possessed a copy of this particular family photograph. Thamma, Dadu, Ma, Baba, Kakamoni, Kakima and chubby-cheeked five-year old Jhinuk. It had been taken right after Kakamoni's wedding – in the balcony of their Charu Market house. The balcony in her dreams! All the faces in that photograph had changed. Ma had grown plump, Kakima decidedly thinner, Kakamoni's lively face looked aged now. Baba looked almost the same, yet the image in the photograph was somewhat different from Baba in person. It was amazing how the same time span had transformed the people in the photograph in different ways. Would they return to those old faces in the photograph if time flowed backwards? Jhinuk felt a shudder go down her spine.

Her meditation over, Mrinalini asked, "Want some tea?"

"No," Jhinuk's voice broke. "Come and sit next to me for a while."

"Why don't you have some! If you do, I can make myself a cup too, and indulge in my addiction." Mrinalini hurried out of the room. Jhinuk came and stood in the balcony. Light streamed out from a room behind her and lit up a portion of the empty, silent veranda. The rest of it lay shrouded in a haze of mystery. Thamma soon returned with two cups of tea. The healthier among the inmates did their own work. They shared the cooking and cleaning among themselves. Nursing the sick was a shared labour too. Mrinalini had made these rules.

The two of them sat on cane chairs next to each other. Jhinuk rested her head on Mrinalini's shoulder. Ahhh! The same fragrance once again. Tunir hadn't had the opportunity to meet Jhinuk's Thamma. Poor chap!

"Tunir will come and meet you shortly," she said.

"Huh! I don't think he will. You must have presented an intimidating image of me and put him off! Must have told him I was an old, ill-tempered woman. And cantankerous too."

"You aren't bad-tempered or cantankerous," Jhinuk's voice belied a hidden grief. "People have been using those adjectives with reference to me for the past few days!"

Mrinalini placed her hand lovingly on Jhinuk's head. "Touch wood! Who has been saying such nasty things about my lovely granddaughter?"

"Oh, everybody. My colleagues at school. My friends. Not just that, they keep saying that I've turned macho as well!"

"What do you feel about it?"

"I don't know. I'm not sure. Have I changed a great deal

Thamma? Or, is everybody else wrong?"

"Why should they be wrong?" Mrinalini's smile died. "They judge by what they see. Most people have an angular, partial vision – their sight narrowed by preconceived notions and prejudices, which are hard to shake off. They stick to the body like scales. And our lives are little pools of water where we frolic – like fishes. We are unable to accept new images – things outside the ordinary – visions that are unusual. We charge blindly at them, like the stubborn, single-minded rhino. Mark them with personal prejudices and declare them proper or improper, manly or feminine. Haven't you read the story of Joan of Arc? She was burnt to death by the people she fought for!"

It had begun to drizzle lightly outside. Rain was accompanied by erratic blasts of wind. The tingling from the pain within Jhinuk lessened by slow degrees. "But I'm not Joan of Arc, Thamma," Jhinuk said. "I'm an ordinary girl. Ma says I go overboard with my 'masculine' ways while Baba never wants me to do things my way."

"Are parents supposed to dictate their childrens' likes and dislikes too? They might direct their children for a certain length of time. Everyone has the freedom to choose one's way of life." Mrinalini's voice sounded uncommonly harsh, "My sons freely chose to be what they are today. And just because you're a girl why shouldn't you be allowed to think and act on your own? Remember, you are what you are! It's important to be true to one's self."

"Were you true to yourself all your life Thamma?"

"No. If I did, would my children continue to live their lives bound within fixed limits? There must have been a lot of void in myself too!"

Jhinuk remained silent. All living things prefer to keep within known limits, to remain snugly buried in their own burrows. How many of them actually venture out!

Mrinalini pulled her granddaughter to herself. "What has your Tunir been saying? What does he want?"

The leaves of the mango tree shook in the sudden blast of wind. The wet leaves glistened in the patches of light that fell from street lamps.

Jhinuk shook her head, "I don't know Thamma.

Chapter Twelve

*T*unir lost track of the day sometime during the afternoon. A fax message had arrived around noon – a member of the board of directors had died in a car accident in Bangalore the night before. The news stirred a suppressed holiday mood in the office. Everybody began packing up after a brief condolence meeting. But what could Tunir do with this sudden, unexpected half day that landed from the skies – an unlisted day that he hadn't accounted for. Book-keeping work lay piled high on his table. The day would have easily whizzed past had he sat down at the computer. But probably that would have looked odd on a day like this.

Neelum returned from the toilet to the glass-walled cubicle. She blossomed at the mention of a holiday. Arranging her dupatta across her shoulders, Neelum chucked some papers into her drawer. She turned to face Tunir, "Hi, Tunir! Come on. Let's push off."

Tunir fixed his gaze on Neelum's sparkling brown eyes. "I shall have to. But where can I go now?"

"Wherever you please, to hell if you so desire! Jump off from the second Hooghly Bridge. Roll down the Brigade Parade Ground. Victoria...Victoria..." Neelum occasionally stumbled in her fluent Bengali, groping for the right word. She would then try and express herself through actions. From her flinging arms Tunir understood that she was asking him to crawl up the walls of the Victoria Memorial.

Tunir laughed. "Then? What after I've climbed to the top of the memorial?"

"Have fun with that black marble fairy... but why the black fairy! You have your own fairy, don't you? Brave and beautiful! Ring her up."

Tunir had been planning to do exactly that but he made a show of disinterestedness in front of Neelum, " Well, I might fix up something for myself. But what about you? What are you doing?"

"I'll run straight to Joy's office, pull him out Then...well, a movie perhaps ... anything. What's on at Nandan?"

"No idea! But my dear, suppose your husband refuses to leave office?"

"I shall drag him out. If he dares to refuse, *tangri tor dungi uska* ... I'll break his legs! Will you come with us? Call your girlfriend. We can go to that restaurant by the river, Scoop, and have fun."

"No thanks. Two is company; four a crowd!"

"*Baat mat banao*.* Two is hardly company after a whole year of marriage, yaar! *Sach bolo*,** you want your girlfriend all to yourself right now – your heart is craving for her."

Tunir shrugged casually. The gesture could mean both 'yes' and 'no.'

"Ba...a...ye," drawled Neelum, flying out of the room with a cheeky wink. Tunir stared at Neelum's swinging hips for the next few seconds.

Sanyal in the next cubicle was speedily clearing his table with loud bangs and thumps. The young man refused to stay a minute late in office since he got married. Previously, he would stay back till eight, or even nine in the evening, if Tunir requested. He concocted excuses by the dozen now. Fibbed without batting an eyelid.

Tunir smiled to himself. He dialled Jhinuk's number with the smile still on his face and relaxed his muscles, letting his body sink into the soft, cushioned chair.

Jhinuk's mother answered.

"Is that Tunir? Eh ma! What a shame! Jhinuk went out just a moment ago."

"Do you know where to?"

"Does she inform anyone where she's going these days! She has developed big feet now! She simply told me she would be back by sundown. You were supposed to come over this evening, weren't you?"

---
*baat mat banao..Don't talk rubbish.
**Such bolo..Tell the truth.

"Yes. We had planned something like that."

"I suppose you know that her friend Nilanjana is leaving for Boston, the day after tomorrow? How quickly she managed to get her passport and visa ready! She visited us yesterday with her husband. Jhinuk wasn't at home so she chatted with me. The boy is strange! I didn't find him particularly bright or smart to look at. I wonder how he managed to go abroad! Have you met him?"

Sujata never waited for replies on the telephone. She always carried on with whatever she had to say without waiting for the person on the other end to react. She would continue breathlessly even if the telephone exchange were to tinkle its warning beep for overshooting time. "Hey, you know something? The aedenium you brought me has been flowering! They're such pretty red flowers! Well, they aren't exactly red but a shade of pink. But the flowers are too large for the plant, aren't they? They look a little odd. And here I have Jhinuk's father, who insists that the flowers of the aedenium are a deep scarlet. He doesn't know a thing about gardening and plants! He picked up this information from someone...somewhere!"

Tunir felt impatient. The lady's mind stored up all kinds of information if they didn't meet for a few days! He stopped Sujata rather uncivilly, "Okay, I'll listen to all that when I come. Goodbye."

"Arrey, arrey, one second please! Can you bring me a bird of paradise from Russell Street? Jhinuk says the plant doesn't grow in a pot. I'll have it in a pot and prove my point – Will you?"

"Let me see if I can find one," Tunir clicked the receiver softly back on its cradle. Oh, how she blabbered! Chatter, chatter! The day had turned out to be a rotten one since morning. He had a round of quarrel with Didi just before he left for office. "You have been married off...you should live peacefully with your husband and children, managing your own household and family." But she does nothing of the sort! She is always rushing down to her parents' house, travelling from Moulali to Dhakuria every single day...with fresh complaints! Tries to take over the household! 'Ma, why have you put up those yellow curtains again? They don't match with the walls. Baba, you've been eating rich Mughlai food again! Weren't you suffering from acidity yesterday?' Disgusting! Tanima never acknowledged Tunir's presence in the house! She took undue advantage of the fact that she was five years older.

She arrived this morning without notice and began ordering him around. "You must take Baba to the doctor this afternoon – to his chamber on Dharmatala Street. The appointment with the doctor has been fixed, exactly at four."

She herself would be waltzing off to a party at a friend's place. And Tunir would have to take her orders! Tunir tried explaining that there was nothing seriously wrong with Baba. All men suffered a setback after the golden handshake in office. Baba's illness wasn't physical, but mental. It was a purely psychosomatic case: sudden fluttering of the heart, irritableness, ageing and senility – all were part of the syndrome. Work after all, was the life force for men. What did women know of this! A retired man required an aim and objective in life. He couldn't possibly spend his time doing housework – cooking, cleaning and washing all day, like women did. Even one of those government jobs that Ma had, was not work at all. Knitting and chatting all day and discussing other people's lives! There was a world of difference between a man's working life and a woman's. Even ambitious Neelum prepared shopping lists in office whenever she got the chance.

But would Tunir's sister ever accept that! On the contrary, she said, "Stop that clever patter! Admit that you're shirking family responsibilities."

A bitter fight ensued.

"I don't have the time," Tunir returned. "My job isn't like yours – free days for nine months a year. There's a certain amount of discipline in my office. One can't leave for the day at a moment's notice."

"Huh! Doing additions and subtractions...what else is your job! A clerical job. Why brag about it?"

"It's much more responsible work than that teaching job of yours in college! My humble self takes care of the entire accounts in the head office, understand? And who are you to comment on what work I do? I don't have time; I can't go. Period. Did you ask me when you fixed the appointment? Aren't you ashamed of barging into other people's houses and throwing your weight about?"

"What do you mean – other people's houses? This happens to be my home too!"

"Buzz off! It was your home till the day you got married. You had better go now and manage your husband's house; look after your son's homework, keep track of Bijanda's health, cook nice meals for them and drop in at the college once in a while to draw your pay. Your principal has a special eye for women. He almost salivates when he sees one! So you're lucky – you needn't work hard or take regular classes. And I warn you, if you dare come here and throw your weight about in the future..."

"What will you do, you uncultured brute! I wonder how a sensitive girl like Jhinuk can put up with you!"

Nasty words! If their mother hadn't come and intervened, they would probably have caught each other by the hair and fought like they did as children. What did Didi think of herself! Didn't Tunir know that Jhinuk had performed a brave act? And wasn't he happy about it? Tunir wasn't an uncivilised brute of the Middle Ages! He knew how to heartily applaud success in women. Didn't he inform everybody in this office that Srobona Sarkar was his girl? That she belonged solely to him! As for Jhinuk! Was there any need for her to come charging across to their house and show off the medal that she had got from her school? Her social ratings had shot up anyway fighting the gangsters. The exuberance had been waning, but it had been sparked off once again with this fresh boost! Jhinuk had received an award. Well, maybe she had! So, what was the big deal? Why must people remind Tunir about it every time? Hum...m...m folks! In spite of directing sharp jabs at Tunir and praising Jhinuk, turning her into a Bachendri Pal,* one shouldn't forget the fact that Jhinuk would most certainly be under him in bed.

---

*Bachendri Pal, a famous woman mountaineer, scaled the Everest.

Tunir's body turned taut. There had been another incident this morning, right after he left for office. Another bout of hotheadedness. He had been queueing up politely for a share taxi when a middle-aged sly man in a dhoti broke the line and slipped into the vehicle. Tunir's place was taken. Tunir wouldn't let go of the man, the man was equally bent on sitting. As soon as Tunir pulled open the door of the cab, the man inside slammed it shut. Tunir would have yanked that sly cat out, had not the taxi driver said, irritably, "Go on sir, dump it. Why act smart with the 'taski' gate? Take the next cab." People around him immediately joined in the chorus, "Come on, leave him be. You're simply making trouble, we're late! Take the next taxi, it's here already." Tunir had to do exactly that. His head hung in embarrassment. Saala! The sprightly twenty-seven year old accounts manager of Nelson and Berry was made to look like a fool! Like those stupid villains in the movies. Moreover, he reached office seven minutes late. And after all the trouble he took to reach his office, it chose to close for the day! Ms.Bachendri Pal had vanished from home as well. How long would he have to put up with such nonsense?

Tunir glanced at the computer on his table. His face floated up on the greenish surface of the screen. A shadowline of cubicles showed up in the background. Venetian blinds were drawn across glass-paned windows. The air cooler was nestling at the bottom.

Tunir did everything with robotic precision. The office was almost empty of people. Wafts of smooth, ice cool comfort drifted lazily down the glass cubicles of the huge hall. The environment was adequately soporific, if there happened to be no work.

A faint smell drifted to Tunir's nostrils through the thin layer of drowsiness – the scent of sal flowers. Sweet yet pungent. The long strip of metalled road gradually took shape behind the hazy screen of air. Millions of snow-white sal blossoms almost wiped out the blackness of the highway that snaked up to the horizon. Jhinuk was sprinting down the road like a carefree young girl. She stooped, picked up the sal blossoms and ran. She stood before Tunir with her anchal full of heady fragrance. Her nostrils quivered in excitement. Moist droplets twinkled in the cradle of her chin and her thick eyelashes. Tunir tried touching her. What were those fine grains on her face? Perspiration! Passion and longing! Or were they pollen from the sal blossoms! The deep blue sky cast its shadow on her pupils, like an expanse of the Massanjore lake lying like a jewel in the distance.

Somebody coughed noisily. The scene broke, twisting and crumpling to bits. There was no road, anywhere. The sal forest lining the sides of the highway had vanished into thin air. Tunir jumped and opened his eyes. He took long, deep breaths. No, the fragrance of sal flowers had gone too. The strong, chemical smell of expensive, foreign room spray pervaded the room instead. He breathed once again. Why did memories from his college days drift into his office and come to rest by his side!

Tunir stretched and went to the toilet. He splashed water all over his face and neck. And now! What would he do now? He didn't have too many friends. He could perhaps walk down to Dalhousie Square and drop in at Soumya's or Anish's office. Personally, he didn't much enjoy chatting with friends inside their offices. He had turned down a lunch invitation from Soumya last week. Should he, in that case, visit Soumya at office for a chat?

However, Tunir didn't let his face reflect his feelings even on the mirror in the office toilet. He suspected that the mirror would, like a good detective, deftly convey the entire data bank of his innermost thoughts to the management ... like the toilet in Charlie Chaplin's *Modern Times*. Tunir tried his best to show a pleasant face on the mirror. The effort wasn't good enough. He thought about going home for a change! He might even take his father to the doctor, after an hour's rest!

Tunir stopped while returning to his cubicle. A bearer! The finance manager had summoned him. Strange! Rajat Roy hasn't left as yet!

Rajat extended a cordial hand as he saw Tunir. "Hi Majumdar! Come in. Please do! I had been planning to catch you alone over the past few days. Got the chance today. Do sit down."

Tunir raised his eyebrows. "Any problem, sir? The Balasore accounts have been settled."

Rajat lighted a cigarette and handed the king-size pack to Tunir, "It's not that."

Tunir was not a smoker; but he lit up. "Then?"

"What's the hurry? Sit down."

In spite of Rajat being fifteen years his senior, they shared an easy relationship. The office followed the American way of personnel management. There weren't too many prohibitions regarding age and status.

Rajat asked lightly, "Care for coffee?"

Tunir shrugged.

Rajat pressed the bell and ordered the bearer for some, then relaxed and settled down in his revolving chair, stretching his arms. The air conditioner in the room droned away, letting off blasts of cool air. Even then, Rajat had the top half of his shirt unbuttoned. He was particularly sensitive to heat because he drank a lot.

Rajat began to speak slowly, carefully choosing his words, "There's news for you. It's secret, and confidential."

Tunir straightened his spine.

Rajat winked. "Has your better half left? Neelum the Erotica?"

"Long ago," Tunir tried to smile.

"You're lucky, Majumdar. Sharing your room with such a voluptuous lady. Spending almost ten hours a day with her!"

Tunir was watching Rajat. Rajat was a shrewd man. His reactions seldom showed on his heavy-jowled face. He laughed and said, "Do you know in spite of having such a wonderful 'bed partner' her husband goes around with another woman?"

Had Rajat summoned him urgently to tell him this? Tunir put on an expression of surprise. "Oh, is that so? Strange!"

Rajat watched Tunir as well. Measured him up and down. Rajat had no qualms about mouthing obscenities regarding women. Tunir derived some amount of fun from such discussions on other days. He even exchanged a few vulgarities himself. But it was different today. He felt rather impatient.

Rajat put on a deadpan expression and threw him a sudden question, "Remember that matter about going abroad, Majumdar?"

Tunir's heart gave a loud thump. "Yes."

"Your chances are bright. Mr. Jones was all praise for you. He has taken a fancy to you. So, young man – I suppose you'll go if you get the chance?"

Tunir went speechless at this bit of unexpected good news. He simply nodded like a clockwork doll.

"Three years in California. How would you like that, man?"

Tunir wanted to scream out his reply, "That's my dream, sir."

"There's just one little problem," Rajat unbuttoned his shirt further. A good bit of his hairless chest was exposed. "I say Majumdar, I believe Neelum spends a good deal of her time in the toilet? Neena from the reception desk was saying so."

Everybody in office knew about Rajat's womanising. He had lately been expressing a great deal of interest in Neelum. Perhaps, because he didn't get much attention from her.

Tunir replied evasively, "I haven't noticed."

"That's the good thing about you, and the reason why I like you – Even more than that Kuruvilla." Rajat sipped his coffee. "Oh yes, to get back to the topic...the problem is that the director and Kuruvilla are relatives. Not too close, but there's some kind of a distant family tie between the two of them."

Tunir's excitement somewhat dimmed. He didn't have this bit of information.

Rajat derived a great deal of amusement from seeing Tunir caught like a mouse in a trap. "Arrey, cheer up. Kuruvilla has been pleading his case with Menon. But I don't think he can win. I shall throw all my weight behind you. You're far more sincere than Kuruvilla. If anybody goes, it will be you."

"Thank you sir." Tunir tried hard to compose himself and sipped his coffee slowly. He asked nervously, "In that case, can I tell my parents that I've been selected?"

"You will, by and by. Break the news gradually." Rajat laughed, "Do you know how I surprised my wife when I travelled to the States for the first time in my life, in '76? My wife was then my girlfriend. Do you know what I did? I took her straight to the marriage registration office along with three friends. Runa was frightened out of her wits. She kept saying, 'I haven't told my father about this. How can I possibly get married?' I simply tossed her the letter. And the formalities were complete by the time she recovered from her daze. Runa's passport and visa took some time, of course! But that was a real honeymoon! A new country...California in December... snowing through the nights and the days. A snowfall is too romantic for words. Snowflakes landing like soft fluffy cotton ... a blue moon ... By the by, when do you plan to get married?" Before Tunir could reply Rajat suddenly stood up. "Just a minute. I'll be right back." He walked into the toilet.

California loomed large before Tunir's eyes. He was sitting in a glass-panelled room, watching the snowfall outside. Jhinuk nestled close to him, their bodies touching. Jhinuk was recovering from her afternoonitis. The sweet fragrance of sal flowers filled the air of California.

Rajat returned zipping up his trousers. "I think my sugar has gone up, Majumdar. I need a check-up."

Tunir didn't hear him.

Rajat swirled in his revolving chair. "What's your girlfriend's name? It's quite a famous name ... it appeared in the papers ..."

Tunir dreamily replied, "Srobona."

"Oh yes, of course, Srobona. Acchha, Majumdar, what exactly does Srobona mean? Has it got anything to do with hearing?"

Tunir couldn't help smiling. "No. Srobona happens to be the name of a star."

"Oh, is that so? A very appropriate name. She really is a star. I think I've seen her with you – in the first floor of New Empire. Am I right?"

"You've a wonderful memory sir. It was so long ago, but you still remember!"

"Computer memory. I can give you a detailed description. A very sweet lady. Charming. And smart too! Quite daring in fact." Rajat laughed and winked, "A good figure. Lucky dog... you!"

Tunir didn't approve of this last remark. But he still managed to say, "Thank you, sir."

Rajat bent closer towards Tunir. His face suddenly serious, he said, "Let's come to the point. No use beating about the bush. Now listen carefully. The finance director has a proposal. You might say it's a request. Do you know Radheshyam Gupta? R.G.? The renowned promoter?"

~

Tunir's hands shook while pressing the doorbell. How extremely fatigued he felt today after climbing to the fourth floor!

Jhinuk sat in the drawing room, talking to a man. Her eyes lit up like a chandelier as she saw Tunir come in. Not waiting for a formal round of introductions, the man stood up. "I'm Sharat Ghoshal," he said. "I suppose you're Tunir?"

Tired, Tunir slumped on the sofa. "I've heard a lot about you."

Sujata looked crestfallen. There was no bird of paradise in Tunir's hands.

Sharat and Jhinuk had a bunch of newspaper cuttings before them. Jhinuk was boiling with excitement. Tunir hadn't seen such joy, such exuberance in her for a long time. That same face, moist with pollens of sal blossoms. The same fragrance. Tunir's eyes were drawn to Jhinuk, over and over again. This woman – restless and carefree – belonged to him. She was solely his. He yearned to touch her, to feel her.

Jhinuk pushed the bunch of papers away and looked up at Tunir. "What's wrong? Did you get beaten up in office today?" She turned to Sharat. "Do you know Sharatbabu, the finance manager often makes poor Tunir hold his ears and stand on top of the table."

Sharat burst into laughter. "Oh, your grandmother does that to me as well. She makes me stand, not on the table but on the road. Out in the sun. Holding bricks in my two hands."

Tunir tried hard to be his normal self. He broke in, "What is your crime?"

"My medicines take a week instead of the customary seven days to quell the fever."

A hackneyed, rustic joke. Tunir inwardly screwed up his nose in disgust. Ignoring the man, he spoke directly to Jhinuk, "The final decision was more or less made today. I'm going, perhaps in December."

"O-o-ooh, is that so!" Jhinuk sprang up like an excited little girl and flung herself down beside him. "And you've kept quiet about it all this while?"

Sujata rushed in, hearing Jhinuk's joyous voice. Her grief for the bird of paradise vanished completely after she heard it all. A new worry cropped up instead. "I'm not going to listen to your excuses anymore, dear. When should I visit your parents?"

Jhinuk blushed deeply. She glanced at Sharat from out of the corner of her eye and lightly chided her mother, "Why are you making such a scene? You really are a...!"

Tunir was smiling. Sharat stood up. "I'd better take my leave now. Enjoy your little chat. I'll convey both pieces of good news to Mrinal-Ma tomorrow."

Tunir was least interested in what the rustic said. He had taken off his glasses and was busy wiping his face with his handkerchief.

"It's been a truly wonderful day today," said Jhinuk. "You've such grand news and I too have one. Do you know? The police filed the charge sheet yesterday."

Tunir froze in a moment, turning cold like chunks of ice. Jhinuk hardly noticed the change. She was drunk with words today, "Sharatbabu mentioned that such cases usually got early dates – at least with that particular magistrate. Those fellows will now be behind bars!"

Sharat! Sharat! Sharat! Tunir rubbed his knees with fists tightly clenched. Couldn't he possibly hold that man by his neck and throw him out right now?

Sharat stopped at the door before he left. "I presume you'll get your date in September. I'll inform you later."

Tunir was standing in the lonely balcony, alone. Jhinuk walked up to him and stood by his side, "What are you thinking?"

Tunir had his beloved – the woman he adored most – close to his breast and yet the ice didn't seem to melt. He blurted out indistinctly, "Jhinuk, will you promise me something?"

Jhinuk was taken aback like a bewildered doe. "You...! What's the matter with you? What's wrong?"

Tunir's voice shook, "You must give me your word first."

The lights in the compound below had been put out. The kanthalichampa tree stood with its dry branches stretched out in dense darkness.

Tunir leaned against the railing. "Forget that doctor fellow...Sharat...leave him alone. A perfect good-for-nothing, taking people for a ride!"

"What do you mean?"

"Drag yourself away from this case Jhinuk. Stay aloof. Give me your word that you will!"

Jhinuk could hardly breathe. Her voice shook, "Why do you say that?"

Tunir gulped. "Getting yourself so deeply involved with complete strangers in a dirty incident ... it doesn't suit you Jhinuk. It doesn't become you."

The earth stopped moving. The evening froze.

Chapter Thirteen

"*W*here would the woman go without her man?
Her husband is her mate; he is her Lord;
He is the only refuge she knows,
Offer all devotion, rituals and sacrifices at his feet."

The old priest swayed, chanting hymns in a nasal tone from the Satyanarayan Panchali.* Well-dressed women, young and old, squatted on the floor, forming a semi-circle around him. Some rocked to the droning rhythm of the hymns. Most, with their minds wandering, chatted softly with their neighbours. The sofa in the sitting room had been pushed back against the wall to make space for the elaborate arrangements of the Narayan puja. Sundry ingredients were neatly laid out on the blue-black mosaic floor.

---

*Satyanarayan Panchali is the holy book of the god Narayan, worshipped in Bengal.

Romita's mother-in-law, in a grand silk sari, was breathing heavily in the heat. Struggling to keep the straps of her bright red sleeveless blouse in place, she signalled to her elder daughter-in-law to turn on the two ceiling fans.

Romita felt relieved the fans were on. Morning sickness had plagued her for some time. It was almost her fourth month now, yet she still felt sick. The strong fumes and fragrance of burning incense also added to her discomfort. But she couldn't leave the place while the Panchali reading was on. That would have annoyed her mother-in-law, as the puja had been specially arranged for her and Palash's benefit.

The family Guru had stopped for three days at their house on his way from Benaras to Puri. According to his verdict, the house had been made unholy by sinful acts committed in the recent past. He had taken special care to tie a nine-jewelled holy talisman on Romita's arm and suggested other remedies to ward off the evil eye. Romita must feed a handful of uncooked atap rice to the birds after her bath every morning. All members of the family were to eat out of banana leaves and carefully avoid all steel, zinc or glassware – from one full moon to the next. Romita and Palash must abstain from sex on Tuesdays and Saturdays. Besides, she would have to feed a cow once a week with her own hands, for the next three months. It would have to be a cow and not an ox or a bull.

Damayanti whispered into Romita's ears, "Why are you so restless? Feeling sick?"

Romita's tassar silk sari kept slipping off. Tucking the loose end tightly into her waist, Romita straightened her back. "No, I'm fine. What's the time?"

Damayanti was Palash's cousin, his uncle's daughter. A professor of chemistry at the university and about forty-five years old. She had a beautiful mane of hair at the time of Romita's marriage but had recently cut it to a short bob. Her favourite hobby was collecting expensive saris from the different provinces of India. She was clad today in an exquisite, buttercup yellow Rajkot cotton. Her matching blouse had a particularly low neckline. She had recently received holy initiation (diksha) from the Guru. She glanced at her bracelet-patterned Quartz wristwatch and replied, "It's ten past twelve. Are you hungry?"

Romita shook her head. She was never hungry these days, in spite of the doctor showering her with health tonics.

Damayanti moved closer to Romita. "Is it true that the Gurudev has predicted a son for you after going through Pulu's horoscope?"

"Hum...m...m."

Leena was closely following Romita and Damayanti's conversation. She turned back towards them and remarked, "He did if all goes well and the planets are favourable."

A few children came running into the room and ran out the next minute, playing amongst themselves. The chanting was almost over. The priest raised his voice, and addressed the audience, "Chant 'Hari Hari' with all your body and soul. Hari bol. ...Hari bol."*

Everybody stopped talking and lay themselves prostrate on the

---

*Hari bol: Say the name of Hari, another name of Narayan.

floor. A soft murmur rose in the room, "Hari bolo, Hari bolo." In the midst of the murmur, a young girl in jeans rushed into the room.

"Oh no!" she exclaimed in dismay. "It's all over. But mother sent sweets for the offering."

Romita's aunt-in-law looked at her with irritation. "Why are you so late? I had told Rini that the puja would be over by noon. Sit down. Take a sprinkle of holy water."

With some effort, the girl managed to sit crosslegged on the floor. The box of sweets got passed on to the Deity. Romita's father-in-law was at the doorway to receive a sprinkle of the *shantir jol*, holy water, too. Everybody was careful to cover their feet while receiving the water.

The priest was getting ready to leave when Romita's mother-in-law said, "Thakurmoshai, please take a round of the house with Chhotobouma and sprinkle the water in every room. And do save some water in the small pot for my sons."

"Check if Tultuli is okay, when you go," Leena said to Romita. "Call me if she's awake."

Romita showed the priest around the house. She took him upstairs and came down after sprinkling water in all the rooms. Then she escorted him round the ground floor, across the kitchen, the pantry, her father-in-law's study, and down the long stretch of balcony to the front door. A cemented patch of courtyard lay beyond the doorway. The priest sprinkled water there too and came back to say, "There's someone waiting by the door. Go and look, daughter."

High walls encircled the house, with a thick growth of

madhabilata covering the fancy front gate. A middle-aged man in shirt and dhoti stood outside the gate, trying to peep in.

Romita walked up to him. "Who are you looking for?" she enquired.

"Is this 23 B, Golf Club Avenue?"

"Yes. What is it?"

"Do Romita Choudhury and Palash Choudhury live here?"

"I'm Romita. Palash Choudhury is my husband."

"Summons from Alipore Court."

The man with a white stubble under his chin pulled out a bunch of papers from a bag with a broken chain. A chill ran down Romita's spine. For a moment, she thought of calling her father-in-law.

The man handed out two sheets of paper along with a bound, dog-eared notebook.

"Sign here, please. I'm giving you your husband's papers as well."

Romita tried out a faint excuse. "Wait a minute," she said. "I'll go inside and get a pen."

"Do we have time to wait, Didi? Do you have any idea how many summons I've got to serve today?" The man fished out a ballpoint pen refill from his pocket. He carefully rubbed the refill on his sticky, oily hair. "Do you know how people cook up excuses before signing and never come back?"

Romita's nerves were almost numb but she still flared up, "Do I look like I'm going to run away?"

"Can you gauge people simply by looking at their faces, Didi?"

The man put on a deadpan expression. "Take for example what happened on the day before yesterday in Kudghat. A nice-looking lady simply vanished indoors after saying 'Coming.' Five minutes passed, even ten minutes ... there was no sign of her. Finally, as I lost my patience and entered the house, a huge dog – almost the size of a calf – rushed in, growling his head off. My goodness, what a size! Even a tiger would have kept away. I somehow managed to run away and save my dear life ... Moreover, I lost my new ballpoint pen in the confusion."

Romita grew impatient and whimsically put her hand out. "Come on, show me where I have to sign."

The man leaned closer – almost touching Romita's body – to show her the space allotted for signatures. "If you don't mind Didi," he carried on, "there's no harm in speaking out the truth. There are many of us who come to serve court summons but leave without giving them in return for a five-rupee note. I'm not one of those petty pilfering bailiffs, mind you. I'd rather ask you straightaway for some cash if I genuinely needed some. But no illegal business from honest folks like me."

Romita came to her senses after the man left. Was the man asking for money? She wouldn't have had to accept the summons had she handed him some money? But that would have amounted to a bribe! How on earth could she possibly offer money to a stranger? Oh well, now that she had accepted the summons, there was no use worrying about the matter as nothing much could be done about it.

Romita's eyes fell on her father-in-law in his study as she

climbed the stairs. He sat reclining on the easy chair, reading the newspaper. Romita came back to the room with some amount of trepidation even after walking past it. With a trembling voice she called, "Baba."

Romita's father-in-law removed his eyes from the newspaper.

"Baba, someone had come from the court."

"From where?"

"From the Alipore Court." Romita inched closer to him. She gulped and said, "He handed me two summons."

Examining the two sheets of paper closely Romita's father-in-law muttered, "Summons for the two of you to stand witness. The date is September 23. Why did you take this? You could have called me."

"The man caught me unawares ... I ... I couldn't pluck up enough courage ... did I make a mistake Baba?"

"Didn't Pulu warn you about this?"

"Er...I don't think so ... he didn't!"

"Such a callous boy! He's a good for nothing...there's nothing in his head besides foolish thoughts. How many times have I told him... the lawyer took such pains to explain the matter...but still the summons have been accepted! Even you didn't think twice before taking it."

Embarrassed, Romita wound one end of her sari's border round her fingers. She spoke in all humility, "But Baba, one is compelled to appear as witness if there's a call from the court. There is no option."

"The court doesn't call if you don't accept the summons." There was an expression of extreme irritation on her father-in-law's sullen face. "You seem to know all the answers!"

Romita's head hung low.

"Since you've accepted it, nothing much can be done. Go and put it away."

Romita was about to turn back when her father-in-law called her back. "Does your mother-in-law know?"

"No."

"What on earth is she doing? Still chanting 'Hari-Hari' with her flock?"

"Shall I call Ma?"

"Oh, let her be. All women are foolish."

With a pale face, Romita climbed the stairs. The landing of the stairway had a window with a narrow strip of coloured glass pane. It was closed. A streak of blue-yellow light had broken through the pane, and stretched itself out in the darkness beneath the stairway. Romita's shadow fell against the light. The shadow lengthened with every step she climbed. The shadow grew longer as she took another step. A shiver ran down Romita's body. It gave her the creeps even in the crowded house. As though it wasn't her own shadow on the floor but a spectre of her recent past. It would linger on, even if she didn't want it, and would lengthen with each passing day.

Romita ran up the few remaining steps. Sounds of laughter and chatter rang out of the women's domain inside, like the notes of a sitar. Romita turned back to look. The shadow had vanished.

Meanwhile, a group of Romita's female cousins-in-law and

cousins' wives had settled down to a hearty gossip on her bed. As Romita entered the room, one of them sang out cheerfully, "We've taken over your bed."

Romita smiled stiffly.

Another remarked, "Did you notice how nervous she looks? Don't worry, there's Leenaboudi's bed that we can freely take over. She's an old sinner!"

Romita quietly opened her cupboard. Where should she keep the papers? On Palash's wardrobe shelf? No. She opened her locker behind the wide open door of the cupboard. There were a few pieces of jewellery in a tiny jewellery box. She wore them on informal occasions. With shaking hands she slipped the papers into it. Stopping for a moment while closing the door of the locker, she put her hand in once again. She had removed the newspaper cutting from her bedside box and kept it there. Avoiding the prying eyes of people around her, she brushed her fingers against the photograph of Srobona Sarkar now, for even touching the picture revived her. One lone girl blindly swishing her handbag in all directions – Putting those animals to flight!

"Hey, what are you doing with your face in your cupboard?"

Romita closed her locker quickly and sat on the bed. She felt much better, more cheerful now. Flashing a bright smile she said, "Oh dear, don't you know I have my heart hidden in there."

"Inside the jewellery box?"

"Which of your jewels has it? Your diamond nose stud that Palashda gave you on your wedding night?"

Romita pursed up her lips and smiled.

Leena appeared at the door, "Baba is having lunch downstairs. I've made the kids sit down too. We'll fit in some of you at the table on this floor. Do come and eat."

One of Palash's cousin's wives raised the subject during lunch. "Who were you speaking to, next to the gate, Romita?"

Romita was serving food. A good bit of daal slipped on to Romita's mother-in-law's plate from her trembling hands. "When?" she asked.

"Why! I saw you signing and receiving something."

"No, Maladi, you're mistaken." Romita lied withour batting an eyelid, "I had gone into the kitchen after *shantir jol*."

Sharp-eyed Mala was not the kind of woman to accept defeat. Within the family she was reputed to be sharp-tongued. She said,"I had gone to the kitchen to get some fruit juice for the aunts but I never saw you there."

Romita's mother-in-law probably smelt danger. She quickly piped in, "No Mala, Romita is quite right. I had sent her to the kitchen to find out if the snacks were ready to be served."

There was turbulence in the air! Damayanti took control of the rudder and steered through. "Aren't we having fun after such a long time? Whatever you might say, incense and hymns change the atmosphere of a house. It resembles a temple, doesn't it, Kakima?"

"We owe it all to our priest. He recites the hymns beautifully."

Romita's mother-in-law's best friend, the one who was the owner of a beauty parlour, said, "Mantras definitely have an effect. I am planning to start a meditation class at the parlour. Sanskrit hymns will be played softly on the stereo while meditation is in progress. How do you like the idea, Damayanti?"

"Great! If hymns don't have an effect why did the holy men write them out so painstakingly? Evil spirits stay clear of mantras."

The young girl in jeans was scraping the gravy with her long nails. She couldn't keep silent while the elders spoke. "That's exactly what they showed in the film *Payal Teri Kasam* – The tantrik recited mantras in his resounding voice and the malevolent spirits left Amrita Singh and scooted away."

"I think there should be more research on the ancient scriptures – the shastras." Damayanti returned to her own topic. "I was leafing through a paper on Nagarjuna the other day. You wouldn't imagine the amazing work he had done nearly two and a half thousand years ago. Charak, Shusrut, Jeevak – each of them were a genius of Ayurveda. They formulated a vast number of cures from plants. Arre baba, if plants didn't have any use, then why would the Almighty create them?"

"That's precisely the reason I use just herbals at my parlour. Romita had developed such ugly dark circles round her eyes, is there any sign of them now? If I had applied chemicals wouldn't they have spoiled her beautiful skin? And it took just one sitting to clear her sister's face of all the blackheads she had."

"Really Romita has had to cope with such trauma!" Mala had laid her fingers on her favourite subject once again. She put on an innocent expression and gave Romita's mother-in-law a jab with her elbow. "Maima, what became of that case?"

"Oh, who knows!" Romita's mother-in-law gave an evasive

reply, "Pulu and his father have been following it up. They'll know."

Romita's cousin-in-law looked as if she was about to burst into tears. "Isshh, how could they behave like that with a pregnant girl!"

Leena stood with a small bowl full of rasgollas. She quickly said, "No no, she wasn't pregnant then. She had had her...a few days before the incident ..."

One of Romita's aunts-in-law cut her short. "Oh, modern girls like you don't admit a basic fact. The honour of women lies in their own hands. Going to court and publicly broadcasting your shame doesn't increase your self-respect. You should be more careful. Haven't you seen the Mahabharat on TV? When Duryodhan and his men dragged Draupadi to the royal court and disrobed her, all the great heroes were present. But did they protest? How could they? Didn't Draupadi show disrespect to Karna? And didn't she tease Duryodhan? Draupadi had many faults."

"You're right Dida," The teenager agreed, "Rupa Ganguly* behaved abominably with her husbands as well!"

Damayanti snapped back, "Shut up child!"

"Come on, I don't blame Draupadi," said Mala. "It's quite a back-breaking job managing one husband. Must be a lot tougher with five of them around!"

Damayanti said, "Draupadi had some holy feelings still left in herself; Sri Krishna came and saved her. That's precisely the reason I told Romita to ask Gurudev for diksha. She'll be free of

---

*Rupa Ganguly: the actress who played the role of Draupadi.

all feelings of shame."

Leena was serving rasgollas to Damayanti. "Oh yes," she said coldly. "Even ruffians and criminals respect God, don't they? One sniff and they'll know which woman has received diksha. And holy sermons are supposed to rid women of all sins, isn't that so Damayantidi?"

The air in the room turned heavy in a second, adding to Romita's confusion. She had been a religious-minded child, fasting on Shivratris before her marriage, regularly participating in the rituals of Durgapuja and Saraswati puja, carefully reading the Bible in school. Then why did she have to go through this ordeal!

Evening had set in by the time the house had emptied of its guests. The day after tomorrow would be the last day of the month of Bhadra – marking the end of the monsoons and the advent of Durgapuja. Yet, the skies were still tinged with the grey of Shravan and monsoon rains. There was not a trace of the sweltering heat and scorching sun of the afternoon. The sky had turned a pale, slatey grey once more.

Her tired mother-in-law had retired to her bedroom for a much-needed siesta. Her father-in-law was resting in the sitting room downstairs. Even Leena had shut herself up in her bedroom along with her infant daughter. Romita alone was awake in the silent house. Waves of anxiety beat against her heart. Why did she have to receive the court summons? She chided herself for having done so. But did she have an alternative? She had stood quite powerless facing that man from the court. Was she truly powerless or had a small seed of an impossible desire taken birth within the depths of her mind at that moment? A desire to punish those filthy men. A longing to stand before the whole world and condemn the wrong – protest against crimes against women. A wish that was as momentary and flimsy as a soap bubble but, still – a wish. Why, oh why did the longing arise if Romita was so powerless, so utterly unable to keep the speck of desire burning? And why did that desire still simmer within her soul? Torturing her, leaving her singed? Why?

Romita left her bed and stood beside the window. It was raining outside. Water streamed down the bark of the huge krishnachura tree. A dripping dog stood huddled under it, nestling against the thick trunk, looking up with pleading eyes, trying to locate the source of the downpour. The poor dog was wet to its skin in spite of standing under the tree. It tried leaving its shelter and going out in the rain but ran back as soon as the sharp needles of water pricked against its skin. The poor animal would have probably reached a safer and drier place if it mustered up enough courage and left the tree to venture out into the rain. And it would simply get soaked if it did not find a suitable one soon. It was already quite wet standing under the tree which hardly provided any cover. Out in the rain, it would at least have the liberty to enjoy the cold shower under an open sky – a better proposition than its present misery. Romita pressed her face against the window grill and hissed softly at the dog,'Go! Come on, get out." The dog tried to brave the rain once more. The next moment, curling up its tail, it retreated. Romita's voice had evidently not reached it. The dog now stood on the other side of the trunk, out of Romita's sight, bathing in the falling water.

Evening descended fast. Staring at the rain, Romita had not noticed Palash's return. Nor had she heard him walking up and stopping right behind her.

Palash, still in his rain-soaked clothes, put his arms round Romita, startling her. "Is my little princess standing by the window and listening to music of the falling rain?"

"Let go, please," Romita said. "I'm getting wet."

"Oh, do get wet darling. Get soaked. Don't you feel like singing in the rain?"

Romita shrugged him off, "No, not particularly. I don't feel up to it."

"But you can't say that now, my love. I want you, I'm dying to hold you, to love you, now."

Romita closed her eyes. Palash put his arms round her once again, passionately, with a tighter grip. Even the shy and introvert Palash had realised that he was the all-powerful male, the one to decide when he would be a romantic lover, and when a blindly passionate one – forcing his love upon his woman. Or at times, be cold, shorn of all desire, a yogi without emotions. Romita took no part in those decisions. And if she did, it was because Palash desired it.

"Which song would you like me to sing now?" Romita asked dispassionately.

"*E bhora badar, maha bhadar, shunya mandir mor ...*"*

---

*E bhara badar ... A line from the medieval poet Bidyapati, meaning 'the rains have come, the sky is laden, but my heart is empty..'

Romita did not open her eyes. "The summons arrived today," she announced.

Palash seemed to be in a particularly good mood. The promotion file in office had been sent to the Cabinet. He didn't pay much heed to the word 'summons' initially. Instead, he hummed a Ramprasadi tune to himself, replacing the original words with his own, "Wait a moment summons. Let me look at my wife as long as I wish to. And see whether my darling smiles in the evening light."

A wry smile appeared at the corner of Romita's lips and vanished. "Both our summons have arrived from the Alipore Court."

It was as if Palash was whipped upright. "When did it come? When? Who received it?"

Romita opened the cupboard and handed out a dry set of kurta and pyjamas to him, "It came in the afternoon. I took it."

"You took it?"

"The man from the court handed it over to me."

Palash paced up and down, from one end of the room to the other. "You could have turned the bailiff away. Could have denied that Romita Chowdhury and Palash Chowdhury lived here. Or told him that he had knocked at the wrong address."

"That's a lie!"

"Oh sure! You women never lie! I should have remembered," said Palash sarcastically. "Well, if you couldn't lie, then you could at least have squeezed some money into his hands."

Romita looked crestfallen at the sudden sting in Palash's voice.

Her thoughts lay broken, scattered like the wavering image of a face in the mirror of a moving train. "I told Baba I'm sorry that I made this mistake," she mumbled weakly.

"Oh lovely!" Palash mocked at her, almost chewing his words, "You're sorry and that relieves you of all responsibility, right? Where is the summons? Let me have a look."

Palash snatched the papers away from Romita's hands and read. The wet dog out in the street tried once more to venture out from under its tree cover. "If I have to go to court, I surely won't let those boys go scot free. They may belong to respectable families, so do I. Don't I have any social prestige?" Palash burst out.

He glared at Romita, "It's the twenty-third. That's next week." He rushed downstairs without changing his wet clothes.

Romita bent over the railing, trying to get a better view of the floor below. Not a sound floated up. The sitting room wall clock chimed 6 o' clock. Each gong rang loud in Romita's head.

Romita's mother-in-law came out of her room. "What's wrong? Why are you standing here? Has Palash come back?"

Romita nodded, holding her breath.

"Remember to sprinkle the *shantir jol* on him. Why hasn't Mono's Ma served tea? And where is Leena?"

"Downstairs, I suppose," answered Romita absent-mindedly.

"Why don't you go and look. If I don't get my afternoon tea…I already have a bad headache after this morning's fast."

Romita stood still, not moving an inch. Palash was coming up the stairs.

Chapter Fourteen

*J*hinuk lost her patience. "Who are you? Why don't you speak? And why do you keep calling us on the telephone?"

As usual, not a sound from the other side.

"What do you want? You seem to have lost your voice – coward – answer if you have any guts."

The sound of a breath drifted across. Long, and deep.

Jhinuk yelled at the caller, "What do you take me for? Will I curl up in fear if you keep making these calls? Now, listen to me carefully. You don't know me. You can keep harassing me a thousand times ... for as long as you wish. Srobona Sarkar isn't going to budge an inch from her decision. I don't care what you do. I'm not afraid of you."

The receiver began to buzz. The line was disconnected.

Jhinuk banged the receiver down on its cradle. The ghost calls had stopped for about a month in between; they had resumed a week ago. The calls used to come at night before, now there was no fixed time. Morning, late afternoon or evening, the telephone would go jangle, jangle. The line would get immediately disconnected if Manas or Sujata picked up the phone. If Jhinuk happened to answer, there would be a few minutes of silence and then, the ringing tone would come back. Was someone trying Jhinuk's patience?

It was eleven in the morning. Manas' classes would begin late today, he had time to enjoy an early, relaxed lunch. But he had left his unfinished meal in sudden apprehension and had rushed to the telephone. Sujata stood transfixed next to the dining table. Their faces turned pale with fear.

"Did you hear a voice? Did someone speak?"

"No."

Manas' patience was shattered. "We'll go to the police station today," he declared in a bewildered voice. "Come what may."

"I won't go to the thana."

Sujata made a noisy protest, "Why won't you? They're trying to terrorise us the day before the hearing... At first you *did* want to go to the thana!"

"We could at least ask for protection tomorrow. That's important!"

Jhinuk sat down on the sofa. She had been to the thana just two days ago, after school with Madhuri. The new O.C. was terribly uncivil, he didn't even ask them to sit, and he threw vulgar, mocking questions at her all the while. "How did they threaten you? What exactly did they say? Oh, so you heard nothing! Just listened to the sound of the ring! ...And that made you feel threatened enough to come running to the police. The boys have landed in a soup already, madam – do you want to make a mountain out of a molehill and make things worse for them? This is the problem with women. Striding out of the house declaring that they want to be equal to men, but they're always afraid of someone abusing them. Bunch of touch-me-nots! Imagining things even while sitting at home ...! Listen to me madam, this complaint of yours doesn't really fit our bill. You had better go to the telephone office and see ... They could perhaps tell you where the fault lay – in the line or maybe the receiver. Perhaps those buggers have managed to tangle up your line with someone else's ..."

Such an affront and that too in front of Madhuri!

Jhinuk bit her lips hard. Must she go to that horrible man once again? Never. Her last thought shot out as a single word, "Never."

"What do you mean 'never'?" cried Sujata. "How dare you be stubborn? We feel nervous and threatened. We want police protection. And you say that?"

"Look Ma, I'm not scared of going to the thana. Your knees buckled last time, not mine. And now it's you who..."

"Oh, all right. That's okay," Manas tried to pacify the two, "I'm not letting her go to the court alone tomorrow. I shall go with her. And Chhoton has been told about this, he'll arrive tonight. If there are two of us accompanying her ..."

"Come, finish your lunch." Sujata pulled at Manas' arm, "I'll ask Tunir to go along as well."

"Why Tunir? Aren't two bodyguards good enough? Do I need an entire battalion?"

"If we decide to have more than two, that's final." Sujata turned around, "Let's make this clear now. You'll say exactly what Tunir advises you to say in court and not a word more. Don't go blabbing away on your own."

Tunir would decide what Jhinuk would say in court? Jhinuk threw her a sharp glance. "What has the great man been saying, may I know?"

"There's nothing unreasonable or wrong about what he said. He simply said that if it's mandatory then she should go, and repeat what the woman and her husband say in court. Let them stand as witnesses. You can just repeat what they say. This is what happened ... and then that is what actually happened...don't you go and act smart by trying to explain things. Is it your responsibility? Did those boys misbehave with you? Well, you did go and rescue that girl. Wasn't that enough?"

Jhinuk threw a burning glance at Sujata and stomped off to her room. If you let go even a centimetre, people rush ten feet into your territory and grab the rest! Parents, brothers, sisters, everybody! The moment Jhinuk forced herself to agree to being escorted to court by her father and brother, she was under another pressure! She would have to act according to Tunir's wishes and do as she was told! Damn it, was Tunir Jhinuk's master?

The backdrop of trees was swathed in a deep green. The undergrowth encircling the trunk of the coconut tree formed a fresh green cluster. A couple of white kaash blooms swayed tall above the thickets. Fluffy white clouds of autumn floated listlessly in an azure sky. The tiny pool was brimming with olive green ripple, fragments of clouds lay reflected in water.

Jhinuk couldn't stay still. It was a waste of two free days. She should have taken just tomorrow off. She moved away from the window. There was an injured snake, secretly rearing its head up somewhere deep down within her ribs! Why did Ma have to speak about Tunir all of a sudden? Had Tunir told Ma something confidentially? Had there been a secret discussion or a deal between the two? Strangely enough, Tunir had been silent and withdrawn with Jhinuk for the past month. He had held back right, after the day he behaved so mysteriously about the court case – had been inattentive and preoccupied, distancing himself from her – looking up to the sky at the mention of Sarat Ghoshal's name, staring absently at flowers and birds. Even on the day she asked him to go and visit Thamma, Tunir had remained silent, cracking open groundnuts and popping them into his mouth in clockwork motion. And he would lose his temper at the slightest pretext. Jhinuk had reached the movie hall ten minutes late last Sunday. Tunir had sat fixed as a wooden idol through the entire film. Jhinuk couldn't bring herself to utter a single sentence. Even a slight touch of her hand made Tunir recoil in annoyance. He would often ignore Jhinuk – a two-legged living, breathing creature – walking beside him down the road. 'For goodness sake, what *is* the matter? Can't you be open about it? Office blues? Your father unwell? Any problem regarding your trip abroad? Or about the court case? Can't you be clear about it and shrug off the bee in your bonnet? Why must you conspire with my mother, instead of sorting out the problem with me!' Possibly the issue of Jhinuk's fight itself had built an iron wall between the two of them! But could small misunderstandings, as these, create such a sea of distance between those in love? Yes, Jhinuk was a little obstinate, hot-headed, a firebrand fighter. But Tunir knew about it, didn't he? And what about his careful, calculated climb up the social ladder? Love had blossomed in spite of their differences! None of them was unreasonable, so why couldn't Tunir openly discuss his secret, gnawing pain with her? Without faith in each other, how could love take root?

In the afternoon, Jhinuk went out without telling Sujata. Walking up to the tram depot she stood there for a while. Then she started walking once again, as if in a trance. Later on, she was rather surprised to find herself in the Metro station complex. How long had she been roaming around the station foolishly, like one possessed? She tore open the wrapper and absently popped a bubblegum into her mouth. There were those stairs from where she had almost jumped down that night. There, to her left, Romita had stood huddled in a corner. And there was the spot in front, where the man in the black T-shirt had wrung Jhinuk's hand. The motorcycles had stood in a line right over there. The hot afternoon air lent a third dimension to that fateful evening. Criminals were known to return to the place of crime. But Jhinuk was not a criminal. This was possibly a different kind of guilt that had shaken her. Was it guilt, or a sense of obligation?

Jhinuk raced down to the bus stop. She would go to the court right now. Sitting down with Robin Dutta was necessary as well, she realised. The seasoned defence lawyers must not have a single opportunity to make easy prey of her at the hearing tomorrow.

Jhinuk was rather disappointed on reaching the court. Robin Dutta was busy talking to a couple of public prosecutors. Sharat was not in his seat. Robin Dutta spotted Jhinuk and asked, "Can I help you? Sharat is away on a five-day leave."

Jhinuk forced herself to put on a pale smile. "I've come to see you."

"Oh yes, certainly." Robin turned all his attention to her, "Your case is due to come up tomorrow. Have you received the summons?"

"Yes."

"Please sit down. Let me wind up this case of weights and measures."

Jhinuk settled carefully into the rickety chair. The two freight officers were busy pointing out something to Robin, from an open green, bound book. With his eyes still on the pages of the book Robin called out, "Sushil, send me four cups of tea. 'Special', please."

There wasn't a chaiwalla in sight. But in a little while a small bare-bodied boy appeared, with a kettle and some cups in his hands. Jhinuk looked at Robin with admiration. Did the man have an intercom fitted to his throat?

The two rough-looking men glanced at Jhinuk out of the corner of their eyes before leaving. Jhinuk spread her odhni neatly across her kameez.

"I came to discuss tomorrow's case with you."

"Do you remember all the details well? The date? Time? Situation?"

"Yes, I do. But this will be the first time that I shall be appearing in court…they have reputed lawyers…"

Robin shrugged off Jhinuk's fears, "Oh, let them," he scoffed. "You must remain firm, and everything else will be fine. Answer my questions carefully and correctly – that itself will help our case."

"No, what I mean is…I feel a slight uneasiness, that's all." Jhinuk tried to sound cool and relaxed, "Why did Sharatbabu suddenly take leave? Is he ill?"

"Do you think any disease will ever catch up with that crazy fellow?" Robin stretched and lit a cigarette. "Don't you know about the dream plans of his ashram? He has been on his toes with that project, travelling quite a bit."

"So the work has begun?"

"No, it hasn't. But when that crazy man has planned it, he will definitely begin work shortly. He's a rather interesting character. I would have written a novel on him, if I had known how to."

Jhinuk said pleasantly, "Yes, I know. He used to teach in a school, and he practises homeopathy as well. Social service is a sort of hobby with him."

Robin screwed up his eyes. "Hasn't he told you anything more?"

"Is there anything else?"

"What do you mean? What little you know is just the tip of the iceberg." Robin rubbed his foot against the cigarette stub and put it off. "He didn't come here immediately after giving up his teaching job. He had settled in Canning and taken up a sarengi's job in a boat. He had even married a local girl from a poor family."

"Oh really? Is Sharatbabu married?"

"Yes, but he's a widower." Robin leaned forward. "A very sad case. His boat developed a snag at Gosaba one night and Sharat couldn't return home. His wife who was alone, was brutally raped that night. She committed suicide a fortnight later."

Jhinuk was struck, as if by a sudden flash of lightning. She stared wide-eyed at Robin Datta.

"Sharat of course, left the place after the incident and moved to Calcutta. Initially, he found himself a clerk's job with a High Court lawyer. Later, he took the law exam. Finally, this job. That too, was pretty long ago ... well, fifteen years at the least." Robin Datta looked the other way. "The bench-clerk next door comes from Canning – heard it all from him."

Jhinuk sprang up like a woman possessed. Her head seemed empty. The bustle of life around her, Robinbabu as he sat facing her, tomorrow's case, Baba, Ma, Thamma...her mind had been wiped clean of everything. The depression that Tunir had caused, that had slowly clouded her mind, her mental tumult over the court case – all had been reduced to insignificance compared to the deep, raw wound that the crazy man bore in his heart with a smile. *She was brutally raped*!

"Please be here by ten tomorrow," Robin reminded.

Jhinuk had turned deaf to all sounds. She somehow wobbled out of the court room and started walking. Aimlessly. She kept on walking.

The afternoon sped on. The evening too. Jhinuk trod homeward through the darkness – pulling her tired legs up the stairs – dragged herself up to the front door, where she froze. Tunir sat on the sofa, flanked by her parents.

Sujata started up at the sight of her daughter. "What's wrong, dear?" she asked in bewilderment. "Why are you in such a state? Where are you coming from?"

Jhinuk had no wish to talk. She flopped down on the sofa. Manas looked extremely worried. "Did anything happen on the road? Jhinuk, why don't you speak?"

Jhinuk shook her head, her face was drained of all colour. "I'm tired," she muttered. "I don't feel too well."

"Did you go to court this afternoon?" enquired Sujata. "Tunir told me that you came out of the court around three o'clock. Where have you been all this time?"

Jhinuk was rudely jerked back to reality. How did Tunir know? An old suspicion knocked at her mind once again.

"Did you simply *have* to go out today? The poor boy has been sitting here all day, waiting for you ever since..."

Even the most innocuous words from those we love take on a bitter note at times like these! Walking towards her bedroom Jhinuk said quietly, "Please call me before you leave Tunir. I've something to say."

Once inside her room, she turned the fan on to full speed. She didn't switch the lights on. The afternoon's lush, verdant world that lay on the other side of the window had taken cover under a film of black soot. The coconut tree stood dark and tall outside. The same tree that stood ramrod straight in her dreams, that seemed to stare at Jhinuk, through the veil of darkness.

Jhinuk was shaken out of her stupor all of a sudden. There were lights. Tunir. Jhinuk sprang to her feet. "Let's go downstairs. Baba and Ma are around."

The two stood near the gate of the compound. Next to a silent, dry kanthalichampa tree. A gentle wind rose, moist from the season's last rains.

Jhinuk's voice was low and fraught with suspicion, "How did you know that I'd been to the court today?"

Tunir seemed well-prepared. "Someone from our office saw you."

"Who was that?"

"Do you know everyone in my office?"

"Oh splendid! I don't know him, yet he seems to know me!"

"He's seen your picture in the papers."

"He remembers a four-month old newspaper photograph? I must say his memory is rather sharp. Where does he live? Introduce me to him. Come, let's go right now."

"Don't you believe me?"

"Is there any reason to believe you? Your eyes clearly say that you're lying."

Tunir's jaws tightened. "You're insulting me!"

"Haven't you insulted me? You've been sucking up to Ma behind my back, discussing my personal affairs with her. Now, what would you call that?"

Tunir remained silent, standing with his hand on the compound wall for a few seconds. Then he shrugged and said, "Okay, I'll tell you. I had made a request earlier, expecting you to stop and think over. But you didn't care. You simply didn't pay heed to my request!"

"But why on earth did you make such a request?"

"I'll tell you why – The father of one of those boys happens to be a close friend of my finance director. Rajat has taken me to Radheshyam Gupta's house as well. And I've talked to that boy Rakesh. He's really sorry for whatever happened that night, presumably at the heat of the moment. Perhaps he had fallen into bad company. He's been punished enough for what he's done. He has spent two weeks in the lock-up! Radheshyamji is almost mad with worry. He's extremely angry and upset about it all. Been very harsh with his son. Just about spared him the rod. You see, this boy belongs to a good, respectable family. You can't possibly expect him to serve a term in jail, can you? Think about it."

It seemed that Tunir was struggling to explain the problem to himself, to his own conscience. Jhinuk was struck dumb. "Are you trying to plead on their behalf?" she forced herself to ask, struggling with each syllable.

"No. I have some obligations as well. Certain personal interests. Well, not solely my own, but concerning both of us." Tunir had brushed off his initial hesitation and indecision. "The finance director and the finance manager will do anything to send me abroad. Can't I keep a small request in return for their interest in me?"

Did the wind suddenly drop? And the streetlights dim to a pallid gloom?

"Don't call it a request," Jhinuk muttered softly. "Admit that it's a deal."

"Oh! That depends on how you look at the proposal."

"Have they appointed private detectives to keep track of my whereabouts? Are they trying to scare me with those ghost calls?"

"Of course not! How could you think of that? They genuinely appreciate what you did that night. Praised you a good deal to me. Even Radheshyamji. But you do understand that they are a wealthy family with a lot of power and social influence…they keep an eye on every little thing, keep a close watch on the police and the thana as well…"

Jhinuk straightened herself. "What exactly do you want?"

"Well, I've told that to you – a girl like you shouldn't be involved in this filthy mess." Tunir touched Jhinuk's hand lightly. "We could be in California this winter, spending a heavenly December and January …! I could guarantee that for the next three years!"

Jhinuk sprang away from his touch. "How could you even think that I would agree to go abroad with you under the circumstances? I'd rather go to hell. Am I going to commit another crime while trying to fight one?"

"What crime? I've had a word with Palash Chowdhury too. Yes, I. Myself. He is under tremendous pressure too. There's his social prestige as well. They are not at all eager to prolong this case and dig their hands deeper into the slime."

How could Jhinuk possibly explain to Tunir that the case was not just Romita Chowdhury's personal issue now. Well, not anymore. There were bigger questions involved. The issue had now acquired a wider dimension and significance. It raised the question of a woman's right to fight for a cause in the present social environment. It didn't really matter now what Romita or her family said or believed.

Jhinuk sighed. "That's not possible anymore. I'm bound by my own conscience. There's no going back."

"Not even after giving a thought to me and my cause?"

Jhinuk blinked back tears. "Please don't make me weak. Let the whole world go its own way, you stay by me – Please Tunir, please – Give up that job. You're efficient and qualified, you'll get better jobs here. Going abroad won't be a problem for us, I'm sure – and must we go abroad? Would life be meaningless if we don't go abroad? Let's settle down here, in *this* city. Lead a clean, honest life, a life with a mission, what more could we want?"

"Even cows and sheep lead a reasonably clean, honest life, don't they?" Tunir sounded sarcastic and impatient. "You must remember the proverb, 'Behind every fortune there is some wrongdoing.'"

"I don't believe in fortune. And I'm not particularly interested in a partnership of crime." Jhinuk struggled to control her emotions,

"Did you know that Sharat Ghoshal is building a home for destitute women out of his own savings? Did you know that the man's wife was raped? I've lost my cool since I heard it…"

"That's exactly what happens when you're bent on making others' lives difficult." Tunir sounded composed and complacent, "Rajat was telling me the other day that those men could even pick you up from the road and rape you. They have the muscle power and the right connections. They will definitely not let you go, if they land up in jail because of you."

"If that happens you'll be next to me – you'll fight. We shall both fight together. Will it hurt to live with a raped wife? Tar your social prestige and respectability?"

"Don't talk rot," Tunir snubbed Jhinuk, stopping to think. He spoke out in a cold voice, "Okay, let's also make deal. I'll do as you wish. Give up that job, and not go abroad. You too must honour my wishes. Just repeat what Palash-Romita say in court. Nothing more, nothing less."

It was a despicable manoeuvre to trade a perfectly legitimate action for a wrong doing. A clever way to satisfy one's ego. Jhinuk couldn't take her eyes away from Tunir. Was this the Tunir she knew? The same boy who came and sat mournfully by her bed while she was down with jaundice! And the one who wrote a seventy-three page love letter, repeating the same words over and over again in each line 'I can forego this world, sacrifice everything to be with you!' Was it the same person who now tempted her to drink poison, assuring her that, in return, he would reject his stolen sweetmeat!

Jhinuk looked at the dead kanthalichampa tree. "Suppose I don't agree and don't strike this deal with you?"

"I shall have to think along different lines in that case." Not a muscle twitched to change his expression. The claws of his raw male ego were out – sharpened and deadly. "Perhaps I shall have to step out of this relationship then. I can't possibly tolerate so much insolence and arrogance even before I begin my life with a woman."

The primitive male stood naked, bared to the skin.

Jhinuk stepped back haltingly towards the stairs. Tunir was slowly becoming a hazy shadow before her tearful wet eyes. "Go away, and don't ever come back to me. Never."

Tunir continued to follow her. "It isn't good for a woman to be so haughty, Jhinuk."

Jhinuk vanished into the darkness.

Chapter
Fifteen

"*I* shall speak the truth and nothing but the truth."

"Your name?"

"Romita Chowdhury."

"Husband's name?"

"Palash Chowdhury."

"Address?"

"23 B, Golf Club Avenue."

"On May 23, at 10 pm, you lodged a FIR at the Tollygunge police station. Right?"

"That's right."

"On that same night, at 9 p.m., four youths attempted to molest you at the Tollygunge Metro station – that was what you stated in your FIR. Right?"

"Yes."

The courtroom was crowded with onlookers. Most of them had turned up to have a look at pretty Romita Chowdhury. Their furtive glances made her smart. Romita hung her head and pulled the end of her sky blue pure silk sari around her shoulders to cover herself.

"Tell us – don't be ashamed – Did they manhandle you? I suppose you'll be able to identify the boys who had behaved indecently towards you –that evening."

Romita kept silent.

"Please look at the witness box and see if these were the boys who had accosted you."

Romita's head hung low, her chin almost touching her chest. It was apparent even from a distance that she was trembling uncontrollably. Robin Dutta spoke in a softer tone, "Don't be afraid. Please look at them."

Romita gave a quick glance and lowered her eyes. It seemed as if the four faces touched her in a flash. Intense anger shook her body, and the next moment she felt faint, her legs almost giving way, the witness box misting before her eyes. Romita tried to pray, her lids closed. "When I pass through the shadowy Valley of Death, let my mind be without fear, O Lord, as You are with me, always… When I… When I pass through the shadowy Valley of Death…" Romita clutched the railing of the witness box to steady herself.

"I don't recognize them," she whispered.

"Don't be nervous Mrs. Chowdhury. Look at them once again. Look straight. Do you know them?"

Romita did not look up. She tonelessly repeated what her father-in-law's lawyer friend had carefully tutored her, "It was a dark, stormy night, with hardly any street lights. I couldn't see the faces properly."

Romita's voice had reached fathomless depths. It shook as she spoke. Did the child in her womb move too? Did it hope to hear something different from its mother?

The public prosecutor was visibly excited, while his clients smiled wryly. The courtroom buzzed with speculation. The murmur gradually wafted out of the room, and the leaves of the ancient banyan tree outside drooped in shame, as they had drooped many times before. A timid dog had curled up under the tree – to get drenched all its life.

Jhinuk stood in the narrow, crowded corridor in front of the courtroom. Manas and Chhoton were with her, while Palash stood at a distance, consciously trying to avoid her eyes. She too, showed little interest in him. A storm was raging in her mind since last night. Jhinuk would have to put her signature on an unwritten agreement if she had to hold Tunir's love for her. Men can't handle personal conflicts and tensions in life without becoming a Duhshasan* or a Ramchandra.** Some try stripping women in public; others ask their beloved to walk through fire. As though a woman was a mere commodity, solely a possession. A woman was expected to be modest and servile if she wanted to be loved

---

*Dushashan, in the *Mahabharat*, disrobed Draupadi in public to humiliate her.

**Ramachandra, in the *Ramayana*, made his wife Sita undergo trial by fire to prove her innocence.

forever. Only then would the deep bond between man and woman remain unbroken. Love was indeed cruel!

"Didi, are you feeling sick? Would you like a drink of water?"

A single sleepless night had produced dark circles under Jhinuk's eyes. She wanted to ask her brother exactly how much water was needed to cool her smouldering heart. Her dry, lifeless lips moved instead, "I don't need it."

"Jhinuk, you're being called inside. Let's go," said Manas.

Jhinuk stopped short of the courtroom. Romita was leaving the room escorted by two gentlemen. Her fair skin had turned a blackish-blue in intense agony. She fixed her sorrowful, helpless eyes on Jhinuk.

Jhinuk's nerves sprang to life at once. Recovering her old determined self, she walked up firmly to the witness box. Her face looked bright and expectant; her voice was bold and clear. Nobody would ever guess that a few moments ago there had been a tumultous upheaval in this girl's heart. She went into the smallest details while describing the incident and answering the queries of the public prosecutor. She depicted each action methodically, pointing at each of the convicted men individually. It was the defence lawyer's turn after Robin Datta had given a sigh of relief and sat down. The defence lawyer was as old as Manas himself, probably older, with a fat, fleshy face, a permanently sweet smile and eyes that dripped with kindness. The man began speaking to Jhinuk in an amiable manner, "Yes dear, please tell me the exact time when the incident took place."

Jhinuk repeated the time once again, "Around 9 p.m."

"Did you reach the spot right then, dear? Or had you been waiting there for a while?"

"I got stuck in the rain after I got off the train."

"You mean you were still on the train when it began to rain?"

"Yes."

"You were alone, I suppose?"

"If I wasn't, then my companion would have definitely gone to the police station with me!"

"Give a clear-cut reply, dear. Were you alone that night?"

"Yes I was."

"Do you frequently travel alone by the Metro at night and alight at the Tollygunge Metro station?"

Robin Dutta jumped to Jhinuk's rescue. "Objection Your Honour. This question bears no relation to the case."

"Objection sustained. Please go on to your next question Mr Mullick."

The lawyer put on a benevolent smile. "Right sir. Yes dear, answer this one question – Do you usually travel alone?"

"Well, sometimes. I have friends travelling with me, too. And relatives."

"Ah, friends? You mean just girlfriends? Do you have boyfriends as well?"

"I happen to have all sorts of friends."

"Are boyfriends more in number than girls?"

"I've never counted," Jhinuk replied grimly.

"Kindly note down Your Honour, Ms. Sarkar is unable to count the exact number of boyfriends she has!"

Robin Dutta sprang up once again. "Sir, I don't understand how these questions are related to the case in hand."

"Oh you will, soon enough," the defence lawyer said in a low voice. He turned to Jhinuk once again, "So dear, you often travel alone. I suppose nobody has ever tried acting funny with you in a similar manner!"

Jhinuk frowned in annoyance. She quipped, "If they did, I would have met you earlier in court."

There were waves of low laughter in the courtroom. The defence lawyer too laughed. "Good! That's like a sensible girl! So dear, you've just mentioned that you often use the Tollygunge Metro station when you return home. Have you ever faced any untoward incident yourself?"

"No."

"When you're alone?"

"No."

"When it's quite late at night?"

"No."

"When you take a stroll around the station complex?"

"I've told you, no. Why do you keep repeating the same question over and over again? I've often waited half an hour at a stretch at the station – nothing has ever happened to me."

The defence lawyer was extremely satisfied at Jhinuk's impatience. "Sir, please note," he said, "She often wanders about the Tollygunge Metro station, alone, even at night. And sometimes she is there for half an hour or even longer."

"I protest sir. The defence is unnecessarily vilifying my witness."

"When have I done so? I merely asked Sir to note down what she said."

"Objection overruled. Please continue."

"Yes dear, tell me now. At what time did you say the incident took place?"

"I have told you. Nine o' clock."

"Weren't you wearing a wrist watch?"

"I was, but I didn't look at my watch when it happened."

"So you must be guessing the time, right?"

"Why should I guess? We went to the police station after twenty minutes or so. That was around quarter to ten."

"Why 'around quarter to ten?' Why can't you be certain? Didn't you look at your watch even then?"

"Yes I did. But I don't remember the exact time. The time has been noted in the FIR."

"Good. Where were you returning from, by Metro, so late at night?"

"Once again, I object, Your Honour. Why does he keep insisting on the lateness of the night? Nine o' clock in Calcutta is by no means late, especially in summer."

"Sir, if our learned public prosecutor keeps protesting at every little thing I say, then it becomes rather difficult for me to carry on with my questioning. If I'm not allowed to refer to night as night, it's a little strange isn't it? Okay, I'll cancel the word 'late.' Now tell me, where were you coming from at nine o' clock that night?"

"From a friend's place in Bhowanipore."

"A boyfriend? Or a girlfriend?"

"A girlfriend."

"So my dear, is the bus stop closer to your friend's house, or the Metro station?"

"Both."

"Okay. You mentioned that your house was in Chanditala. There's a direct bus to Chanditala from Bhowanipore, isn't there?"

"Yes, there is."

"How do you reach home if you take the Metro?"

"I usually take a rickshaw from Tollygunge station. At times, I walk."

"So, it seems that you can reach Chanditala directly if you take a bus. On the other hand, if you take the Metro, you have to climb down to the station and buy a ticket – that takes time. Then again, you have to take a rickshaw home from Tollygunge station. Am I right? Well dear, at what time did you leave your girlfriend's place?"

Jhinuk thought for a few moments. Was it twenty past eight? Half past? What should she say? The words slipped out of her mouth, "Half past eight, I think."

"Guessing again? Fair enough. You have a habit of guessing, I see. Okay, tell me something and try not to guess this time. Are the buses crowded at that hour?"

"Not too crowded."

"It's easier for you to take a bus, cheaper too. Yet, you took pains to take the Metro and to be present at the spot of the crime at nine o' clock sharp! Isn't that too much of a coincidence my dear?"

Jhinuk didn't quite follow the implications of the question, she couldn't think what the answer should be.

"You're groping for the right answer, aren't you?" asked the defence lawyer. "Let me help you. Your presence at the spot of the crime that night was not at all a coincidence. You staged a preconceived, well-rehearsed drama to land these boys in trouble, didn't you? Tell me, am I wrong?"

Jhinuk shook her head angrily. "That's a brazen lie. I don't even know the boys! Why on earth should I try to do that?"

"You don't know them. Yet you identified each of them perfectly well, and with confidence. And you claim that you caught a glimpse of them just once?"

"I had seen them close."

"How close? Were you closer to the boys than the victim herself?"

"No...not really. But, quite close."

"What about the street lights dear? Is the place fairly well-lit at night?"

"Yes, quite."

"And when it's a stormy night, is it still well-lit?"

"Yes."

"But the woman whom you saved from being raped that night, she and her husband, who happened to be there, have both testified that the place had become quite dark because of the squall. Do you think they were both lying?"

"They are afraid of telling the truth."

"Oh, but have they told you that they are afraid?"

"Well, I can guess."

"Excellent my dear. I see that you're not only plucky but gifted with a strong ability to guess as well! Guess! Surmise! Think! Perhaps! Sir, kindly note, she can hardly say anything specific and is here as a witness, on the strength of her ability to surmise! ...Well dear, these four young men facing you, the ones whom you identified so promptly, do you remember how they were dressed that night? Can you describe their clothes?"

"One of them was wearing a black T-shirt, another had on a baggy shirt..."

"Which of them was wearing a black T-shirt?"

Jhinuk was at a loss. She began to perspire. She tried gathering her wits and to think clearly. She tried overcoming her nervousness. "I had seen them only for a few minutes, and was in a state of excitement. It's hardly possible to recollect what each of them was wearing."

"I see, my dear, that your power to hypothesize has diminished after all! Well, you claim to have seen these young men for a few minutes only. But you had seen Palash and Romita Chowdhury for a substantial length of time. Do you remember what they were wearing that night?"

"Palashbabu was wearing trousers. Romita Chowdhury was in a sari."

"What colour was her sari?"

"It was possibly a South Indian – parrot green."

"Again 'possibly'? And what about Palashbabu?"

"I don't remember."

"Strange! You spent a good deal of time with them, you took

the initiative and escorted them to the police station. In spite of that, you don't remember the colour of Palashbabu's shirt! And yet, you seem to know that one of the boys was wearing a black T-shirt?"

"Don't you think that's natural?"

"It's natural only if you had known them well enough. And it's even more natural if you plan to get four innocent boys convicted out of personal vengeance."

"No! They were misbehaving with Romita Chowdhury, pulling her arms, trying to drag her to the motorcycle …"

"You're getting unnecessarily agitated, dear. I never said that there was no attempt at molesting Romita Chowdhury! But these four young men aren't the culprits. If they were, then the victim would have identified them before you did."

"I don't know what the victim has told you. I've come to the court merely to describe what I had seen at the spot of the crime. A motorcycle belonging to one of them has also been found."

"A number of scooters and motorcycles were parked along the kerb that night while it rained, weren't they?"

"Yes, but I gave the number of the motorcycle to the police the same night."

"Well, the particular motorcycle whose number you happen to remember is owned by the young man here! That's hardly proof! Perhaps, the boy had left the motorcycle there before he had gone looking for shelter. Perhaps, you came on the same motorcycle…perhaps, the boy had left after quarrelling with you… Now, now dear, don't get angry! This is a bit like your guessing game. A tiny surmise on my part! Ah, tell me something. You too, are a pretty young woman. Did the boys who tried to molest Romita misbehave with you?" The defence lawyer prodded Jhinuk.

"They pushed me around, threw me down, struck me on my jaws, and twisted my arm."

"Anything else?"

"They used foul language."

"Anything else? Touching your intimate parts for instance…I mean, you are a woman too!"

"No."

"Had you filed a separate diary with the police for the attack on you?"

"No."

"How strange! You were physically assaulted and you didn't report that to the police! Yet, you took the initiative to report someone else's case of attempted molestation!"

"A physical assault on a woman and a…I mean, humiliating a woman…er, I mean…" Jhinuk failed to make her point. Her face was flushed with embarrassment.

Robin Dutta stood up to help her out. "Sir, what she means is that a physical assault on a woman and a sexual assault are not the same things. A sexual assault is more offensive…"

"Yes, yes, we know all that. You needn't lead her." The defence lawyer interrupted, now raising his voice. "But has the physical assault been included in the chargesheet? Under section 355?"

"No."

"Right. I now know all that I need to know. There's just one last question dear. On May 13, at 9 p.m., were there just the three of you at the Metro station complex? Just you, Romita Chowdhury and Palash Chowdhury?"

"No, the place was quite crowded."

"But I don't see any other government witness besides you, dear! Nobody else but you went to the police station?"

"Yes. Unfortunately, the others present at the spot were enjoying the fun, without lending a helping hand. A bunch of cowards!"

"I suppose this must also be a part of you guessing game! My job is done for the moment."

The defence lawyer moved closer to the magistrate. "Sir," he said, "I request you to note down a few salient points. Number one, all the information provided by the witness is based on surmises. She hasn't been able to provide a single, definite answer. Number two, she has countless boyfriends, and she often wanders about the Metro station complex alone at night. Therefore, one should take note of her character and give it a serious thought before filing her statement. Number three, the victim and the victim's husband have clearly stated that since the place was rather ill-lit, they could hardly identify these boys as the culprits, even though they had seen them very closely. As a result, they are not sure whether the convicted young men present here are the real offenders. Number four, the witness has not filed a separate police diary about the physical assault on her. There is not even a medical report! Five, there is not a single witness to the alleged act of molestation at the crowded Metro station besides this lady who relies heavily on her power of imagination! And she happens to be a witness who took great pains to be present at the Metro station at the time of the crime, when she could have easily taken a direct bus home."

The magistrate put away his pen. "You can tell me all this when it's time for the arguments. Do you need to cross-examine this witness any further?"

"Not right now. But I reserve the right to cross-examine her again."

The magistrate turned to Robinbabu, "Would you like to declare the two former witnesses hostile?"

"Definitely sir," Robin Dutta sounded listless. "But I suppose further questioning won't be of much use."

Jhinuk stepped down from the witness box. Dates for the next hearing had been fixed for the coming week. Jhinuk emerged from the courtroom after she had signed her own declaration, feeling weak and faint. Chhoton fetched a glass of water for her. She gulped it down.

Manas put his hand on his exhausted daughter's shoulder. "Go and fetch a taxi quickly," he called out to Chhoton. "We'll come out soon."

The sky was dark with clouds once again. Kites moved in circles, smelling rain after a dry spell, descending earthwards.

Chhoton waited with a taxi in the court complex. "Baba, this way. I'm here," he called out.

A middle-aged gentleman suddenly stood in Jhinuk's way, blocking her path. "I've been waiting all this while to meet and talk to you. You don't know me. I am Romita's father."

Jhinuk looked up blankly.

Manas spoke up, "She doesn't feel too well today. If you could...some other day..."

Jhinuk stopped her father midway,"I'm fine....Do you want to speak to me?"

The tall, sculpted body was hunched. "My daughter failed – I suppose now you won't believe a word I say. But let me tell you that she has been struggling with herself all these months to come out with the truth."

"There was nothing to stop her from saying the truth if she wished," Jhinuk replied, her voice cool and steady.

"It's not easy, my dear. So many responsibilities, obligations and social bindings! I had almost decided to bring her back from her husband's home and say goodbye to her in-laws forever. Throw her sham marriage to the winds! But I couldn't. The girl is pregnant! To be born a woman...you don't know how much she respects you...! She waited all day to hear your voice, to draw some strength and inspiration from you. She would often telephone you secretly from her in-law's house, never gathering up enough courage to speak – however much I tried to reason with her, requesting her to talk to you on the phone, explain her problems, ask for advice, she could never bring herself to do it."

Manas looked dumbfounded. "So it was your daughter who made those calls! But why didn't she speak?"

"In shame and self-contempt!" Tapan's voice broke midway, "My daughter is such a coward! It's my fault perhaps. I have failed to instill a sense of self-respect in her, I haven't taught her how to take a firm stand against any wrong. My daughter doesn't possess the strength of character to protest against injustice. You have it. I sincerely pray that my daughter loses the case, so that you emerge the victor!"

Was this a prayer? A good wish? Or a curse? Jhinuk glanced up thirstily at the sky. The concentric circles of the kites high above had dwindled in size. They had become even smaller. Why hadn't it rained?

Chapter
Sixteen

*M*rinalini was waiting for Jhinuk in the west balcony of Shantiparabar. She looked tired and spent, her worn-out body lay listless on the armchair. Her face was crisscrossed with deep wrinkles. "Come dear," she called out, her voice weighed down with age. She had closed her eyes after spotting Jhinuk.

Jhinuk walked silently up to her and settled down at her feet.

"No, not down there! Get up and sit next to me." Mrinalini said, with her eyes still closed.

Jhinuk did not move. Her hand lay on Mrinalini's knee, touching her lightly. Wasn't it for this much-awaited touch she was driven to this west balcony so often?

The afternoon air bore the fragrance of a crisp sunny autumn. It was Shasthi, the sixth day of the Durgapuja that had arrived relatively late this year. The sky was a spotless blue, without a trace of clouds. The rains had finally retreated after an overwhelming defeat, withdrawing its army of rain clouds a few days ago. Golden sunlight gushed all over, spelling victory. The sound of drumbeats at the Puja mandaps echoed in joyous triumph.

Jhinuk had been defeated. The court case lay deep in its coffin. And the magistrate would hammer in the last nail after the Puja holidays.

Mrinalini touched the top of her granddaughter's head lovingly. "Why do you look so glum dear? It's a special day after all. I've got kheerer chop for you. Come in and eat."

"No, I don't want sweets. I've lost my appetite."

"Your fever has gone down, hasn't it? Why isn't your appetite back yet?"

Jhinuk sighed. It was not merely the taste for food that she had lost – appetite did not lie in the tastebuds alone.

"Would you like something hot and spicy? Shall I get shingaras for you?"

"No, I don't feel up to it. I've given up bubble gums as well."

The fever had pounded her hollow. She had returned home running a high temperature on the last day of the hearing. Her body had been sending alarm signals the day before, during the question hour in court. It burst into a fiery revolt on the third day, while she came down from the witness box, her head held high. The virus raged for a whole week after that, her temperature shooting up to 105 degrees at night. Severe headaches numbed her senses all day, while she lay inanimate like a piece of log. Jhinuk could hardly walk straight then, and had had a bad fall even after her fever had gone down a day before Mahalaya. And her taste buds were still numb. She had no appetite at all.

Jhinuk gently raised the topic she had come primarily to discuss. "Are you actually going to Ramrampur after all?"

"Don't you want me to go? Should I waste the rest of my life here, in this prison? Be a good-for-nothing?"

What did it matter to the rest of the world what Jhinuk desired. She could never hope to achieve it even if she yearned for it all her life! It would be selfish of her to want others to feel like she did. It would also create confusion. Jhinuk spoke with a heavy heart, "If you've already made up your mind, then why ask me? How do I matter? And let me remind you, that it was *you* who had chosen to live in this prison in the first place."

"Don't be silly, dear. Life is always like a prison for a woman. The jailor changes – that's all. He is your father first, then your husband. Perhaps your son next. And sometimes the prison is these walls. The shackles that imprison you, are packaged in a layer of love and bonding. But when the package is undone, the prison at home is more intimidating than the prison here. I'm looking forward to a whiff of fresh air now. Let's see ... I might be able to breathe easy in the new place."

"When are you leaving? Baba was saying that you're actually planning to go immediately after Puja?"

"Precisely. That's what I had in mind. But I still have loose ends to tie up at the bank. My fixed deposit here has to be withdrawn. And merely handing in the notice won't speed things up. Poor Sharat has his hands full. He is floundering with so much to do."

Jhinuk understood the situation but she continued being unreasonable. It seemed Sharat Ghoshal was taking away the only haven she had known in life. "Oh, I don't care," she burst out, her face flushed with annoyance, "Let him suffer. He surely can't hope to escape facing the music if he plans to build ashrams and be a philanthropist!"

Mrinalini couldn't understand the reason behind her granddaughter's annoyance.

"You're right dear," she said. "That's precisely why one needs to go and give him all possible support and help. Did you know that he has already got hold of an orphan and a couple of women deserted by their husbands?"

"Yes, I did," Jhinuk replied drily. "Sharatbabu had come to our house."

"But you promised to help him dear," Mrinalini pointed out. "You could go and visit Ramrampur one of these days. You'll like the place."

Jhinuk kept silent. Her likes and dislikes had lost their edge.

"Would you like to go and see the ashram, dear? If you do I'll ask Sharat to pick you up from home and bring you there. I suggest you go before Lakshmipuja. You'll have your hands full after that. Shopping for a wedding after all is no easy thing! Buying saris, ordering the jewellery…"

"I thought Babli's wedding had been fixed at the end of Magh. Must we bother about the shopping now? And Pishimoni is planning to come only around the end of December or even as late as January!"

"Why should it be Babli's wedding? Your mother came and informed me of your wedding!"

"My wedding?" Jhinuk wouldn't have been as taken aback if the sun had popped out of the sky and landed in the balcony and rolled about the place. "When is the wedding? And who with?" she blurted out, quite dumbfounded.

"Your parents came and told me about it. The date has been fixed as well. They have written to your aunts, asking them to come for the wedding accordingly." Mrinalini watched Jhinuk closely. "But dear, didn't you know? Or are you trying to fool me?"

Jhinuk's nerves were taut beyond limits. Her head throbbed. Staring unblinkingly at Mrinalini she asked, "I've never tried to fool you, Thamma. Never. You had better be out with everything you know. I'd like to know what new conspiracies have been hatched against me."

"Is it true that you don't know anything?"

"Yes it is, precisely so. I don't. Not a word."

Mrinalini rose and ambled down to the far end of the balcony. What she had suspected was true after all. This was the reason why Sujata had held her hands earnestly the other day and entreated her to have a word with Jhinuk. 'Ma,' she had said, 'If you have truly made up your mind to go, please do stay on for Jhinuk's wedding. Suppose we need to talk to her, explain certain things and convince her…if you're not here…you are the only person she listens to…!'

Shantiparabar was rather empty, almost desolate that day. The more kindhearted of the sons and daughters had taken their elderly relatives home for Durgapuja. Prabha Thamma sat in her crisp, new white thaan, staring emptily at the road outside. A coucal called incessantly from the mango tree. A pair of red crested bulbuls flitted about. A couple of trucks sped across the road, drowning the birdcalls with a thunderous roar. The calls returned a few minutes later. Kub, kub, kub, kub – they droned on.

Mrinalini hastily returned to Jhinuk. "The poor boy is heartbroken I hear," she said. "He is very depressed. He has given up his previous job as well…solely for you. He was called for an interview and is supposed to join his new workplace from November. Tunir's sister and brother-in-law came and gave your parents the news, I believe."

"When did all this happen?' Jhinuk whispered to herself in amazement.

"I can't tell you the exact date and time," said Mrinalini. "I suppose it was during your illness. Mantu and Sujata visited the boy's house as well."

Jhinuk sank down on the floor. When did Tanimadi and Bijonda come to see her? She didn't quite remember. Those seven days of her fever still shimmered in the haze of semi-consciousness. Sometimes, fragments of a day surfaced from its dark depths, as short-lived as a flickering midnight star that quickly vanished into the thick dark folds of the night sky. She remembered many of her colleagues among those who had come to see her. Madhuridi, Geetali aunty, Lipikadi and Lekhadi. She vaguely remembered Madhuridi taking her leave application before leaving. Or, was it

Geetali aunty? She was utterly confused. Bishakha, Mainak and Sulagna had come too…Jhinuk groped her way blindly down memory lane. Kakamoni and Kakima had come. Rumki too. Sharat Ghoshal. Babua. And yes, Tanimadi – sitting at Jhinuk's bedside for a fairly long time. Bijonda had stood by the door. Was it that same day…?

Jhinuk had lain exhausted in bed after what seemed like a five-month long marathon! She had run the race, tearing down the last lap, and had finished at the end. She had been repeatedly pushed out of the smooth wide highway track, onto a narrow pointed path edged with thorny and poisonous undergrowth. Her lungs had screamed for the very last drop of air. And the stadium lay deserted, nobody waiting to applaud her. Jhinuk lay in stupor, writhing and feverishly restless, at times with an empty mind. And just then, right in the next room, a meeting was in progress – deciding Jhinuk's fate and a golden future!

Jhinuk felt faint and weak, her knees almost buckling. The fresh wounds in her heart bleeding profusely. Oh, what relentless agony was this!

Mrinalini's hand rested on top of her grand daughter's head. "Steady yourself, dear," she said. "Rest for a while. I feel the boy truly loves you."

"That's a lie. He wouldn't have humiliated me if he did."

"Men don't think and act the same way as women do, dear. They don't realize when they are disrespectful to women. They simply don't have the sensitivity to understand our sentiments. They love women their way, keeping their egos intact."

Mrinalini leaned back against the easy chair. All pent-up passions, humiliations, disenchantments that she had quietly borne through the long years now seemed to rattle her old bony frame. How much of it could she unleash to her dear granddaughter? Could she tell her all, open her heart out, in the space of a short evening?

Her voice shook as she spoke. "What can I say about others? I can tell you about *my* life. Your grandfather had taken a good deal of money from my father as dowry when we got married. That was his demand! But did he ever realize how he humiliated me in the process? What tremendous disrespect that single action had amounted to? I wasn't too bad in studies, you know. But my father married me off just before my matriculation exams. I requested your grandfather to allow me to attend classes after I moved to my in-laws' house. He was a modern young man of those times, so he let me. I matriculated as a private candidate and passed my Intermediate exams fairly decently too. But your grandfather began objecting to my undergraduate studies, saying that it would disrupt home and family life and that our infant son was being neglected. I cried my heart out but he did not relent. His excuse was unfounded though. I used to finish all household chores and sit down to study, with Mantu sleeping on my lap – often at midnight, after the rest of the family went to bed. So, why do you think he objected? It was simply because he didn't want me to be his equal in life. He couldn't risk the possibility of my exam marks being higher than his. Killing my desire to study was an insult, wasn't it? But did it mean that he never loved me? He did. Couldn't spend a day without me."

"Now look, it was I who gave birth to the children. I hope you don't mind my saying this, but suppose I had said that your grandfather was not the parent of your father, uncles and aunts? I was perfectly capable of saying that. And no power in the universe could have disproved me. But we women seldom voice such things. And that's how marriages and families are saved. Well, to sum it all up, a child's mother is the only biological truth. But her wishes and views are seldom considered while bringing a child up. It's always the father who matters. He is the one with the sole right over the child. The mother follows him. Your grandfather too, never paid heed to how I wanted to bring up the children. Whatever he decided was right. It was the ultimate truth. Wasn't that humiliating for me?"

Mrinalini went out of breath after this sudden burst of passionate oratory. Taking a deep breath she added,"I still loved your grandfather however. Love is like that…"

"Are you trying to defend Tunir?" Jhinuk sat up. "Or are you asking me to lose out because you have lost your battle? You failed to stand up against a faulty system so you're probably unable to accept the fact that a girl from the present generation can both fight and win …"

"Oh, whatever you might say," Mrinalini almost snatched away the last bit of conversation from Jhinuk. "I'm not too sure of the changes that might have taken place since our times or how different your times are from ours. Yes, I admit that you are much more at liberty now to lead your life as you wish. Women are joining the army, climbing the Himalayas, educating themselves as much as men, going out to work. But you girls fail to notice a simple fact. Men will allow you only that much ground that they decide to forego. Not an inch more. Men don't like their women sitting bundled up at home any longer. So they have allowed you to educate yourselves. Men can't handle the burden of being the sole breadwinner for the family any more, so they let you work and earn an extra income. You needn't look too far, you know. Look at your own mother and aunts. Your grandmothers before them. You will easily understand how men have granted you 'freedom' step by step over the years. Boys wish to see women in skimpy clothes nowadays. So, you have skimpily-clad women dancing in movies, commercials and television channels – solely to entertain men. And you girls believe this is liberation. This is hardly liberation, my dear. Freedom resides in the mind. And men will never accept a free mind in a woman... Why should they? In spite of being civilized and educated, we still have great faith in the century-old, outdated laws of society. Law lies with those in power, and the powerful survive. Don't you realize this simple truth when you see Romita Choudhury?"

It seemed Jhinuk's Thamma had turned into an angry young woman. Tiny grains of gunpowder accumulated over the years had now shaped her into a massive deathly weapon. Mrinalini sharpened her attacks. "It's not just today's women who can think. Women have always had a head on their shoulders and a capacity to think for themselves. And the strength to protest too. Remember Gandhari, the only person and a woman who protested at the time of the war at Kurukshetra three thousand years ago? And she was the only one who had the courage to protest against Draupadi's dishonour. Gandhari didn't exclude her husband and sons when she cursed the perpetrators of war. She was farsighted enough to perceive more acutely than a normal man even though her eyes were bandaged. She couldn't prevent the war despite being a strong, determined woman. Does that mean Gandhari lost the battle? And was her protest without value?"

Jhinuk managed a pale smile. "No Thamma, a mere protest has no value anywhere. Didn't you notice what a drubbing I got at the court? The defence lawyer roped in a clutch of witnesses who swore that those ruffians were nowhere near the spot of the crime at that time. They even managed to prove that the man whose motorcycle was parked at the spot was actually having tea at a wayside restaurant, about half a mile down the road. The restaurant owner too, swore to that effect, after completing the Geeta-Koran-Bible mandatories. And that lawyer kept pointing at me, openly vilifying me, declaring that I was a liar, a slut, a girl from a respectable family gone astray, someone who walks the Metro stations by night in search of prospective customers and takes revenge on innocent people who refuse to fall into her trap! That lawyer completely turned over the case!" Jhinuk's voice choked with indignation. "Would you still say that protests have value?" she asked her grandmother.

"Yes, I'd say that a thousand times over. It's been your win this time. How many girls can actually fight till the end like you did?"

Jhinuk felt almost prompted to say, 'No Thamma. It was not I who stood erect till the end, facing all opposition alone. It was the tall coconut tree of my dreams. But its trunk had been eaten away by someone gnawing at it, leaving a big hollow inside.' It was someone whom Jhinuk had trusted. She had dreamed of walking a million miles hand in hand with him. He had silently moved over to the enemy camp in the middle of the battle, leaving her stranded. "Are you trying to console me like Sharatbabu did, Thamma?" asked Jhinuk. 'There are always winners and losers in a court case' he had said. 'The victim has unfortunately turned hostile. And the witnesses turned out to be false ones. But all that doesn't affect the credibility of the event in any way madam'... No Thamma, please don't. Not you! Don't ever try to comfort me by such talk."

The afternoon was fading away. The strong sun handed the peach-coloured sky over to the moon for the night. The distant sound of drums and music from microphones drifted into the building, almost trespassing into its silent premises.

Mrinalini rose and switched on the lights in the balcony. Some of the inmates walked out of their rooms and dragged their stiff bodies downstairs to seek the warmth of home and hearth during television time. Mrinalini came back to sit beside her granddaughter after switching on the lights in her room.

"Will you confide in me, dear?" she asked.

"Yes, but about what?"

"You do love your Tunir, don't you?"

"Hmmm."

"Haven't you ever pined for him in the last few days? Didn't you feel like seeing the boy?"

It wasn't Jhinuk but someone else who spoke on her behalf, "Yes, I did."

"Weren't you reminded of the good times you had had together?"

The other Jhinuk kept silent. 'Who would care to rake up the agony that was deep within the heart?'*

"Then why won't you marry Tunir?"

"Look Thamma, who I shall marry or settle down with, is *my* business and will always be. It's my personal affair and I don't want you to interfere. How do all of you matter and why should I consult you? You? Ma? And Baba? Tunir's sister and brother-in-law? Or his family? I happened to have chosen Tunir. And it was *my* decision to marry him."

"Don't say that the decision was solely your own. Both of you decided to marry each other, didn't you? And Tunir still wants you."

Jhinuk's heart crumpled under abysmal pain. It was not anger that she experienced. Its source lay beyond love, indignation or hatred, rooted in the fathomless depths of her heart. "Thamma, tell me something," Jhinuk asked coldly. "Suppose I betrayed all trust and faith in our relationship, humiliated Tunir beyond measure and left him in a wretched condition. Do you think he would have agreed to marry me in spite of everything?"

Her granddaughter's wrath made Mrinalini smile.

---
*This line is from a poem by Jibanananda Das (1899-1954) a famous Bengali poet.

"Don't smile, please," Jhinuk shot back. "Suppose, I had won the case. Do you think Tunir would have come back to me? Would he have left his ego to do that? My defeat has helped him strike a compromise." Jhinuk clenched her fists and added, "I fail to understand a vital point Thamma. How was my wedding fixed without my consent and my knowledge? Didn't they realize that they should have asked me about it? Would anybody have dared to fix Tunir's wedding this way?"

Mrinalini could not provide an answer. There wasn't any.

"Don't keep quiet," Jhinuk retorted. "Are you asking me to spend the rest of my life in subjugation? Like Romita Chowdhury?"

Mrinalini moved uneasily. How could she possibly explain to her grand daughter that she had spent nearly all her seventy years trying to find an answer to these questions? "Life is strange my dear," she muttered in a low voice. "Let me tell you a story that my father often told me. It comes to my mind now, when I'm old and can understand better. A brahmin once fell into a deep well in the forest, his feet and hands got hopelessly entangled in the overgrown creepers and nettles around it. An angry elephant in heat came by and stopped there to stand guard at the opening of the well, while a poisonous snake hissed from below. The brahmin hung upside down, clinging to a slim climber. That wasn't the end of his ordeal, however. A field rat gnawed at the roots of the climber that had flowered profusely. And there was a beehive with scores of bees droning around it. Strangely enough, droplets of honey trickled into the man's mouth straight from the beehive. And the brahmin's thirst for the sweet drops of honey surpassed his fear of death. His thirst remained unquenched, increasing with every drop that fell into his mouth. Human life too, is an enigmatic combination of desperate danger and an insatiable thirst for the pleasures that come with it. It is a fatal attraction that life holds for us. We too, live on the edge of life and death, but our thirst for life's cloying sweetness is never quenched. We live with our greed for the tiny drops of honey that momentarily relieve us of the pain of daily living. Did you follow what I said?"

Jhinuk did. If only it could heal her throbbing pain! If only those numerous instances of humiliation and ignominy that other people had faced, had the power to end her trauma and bring peace to her mind once again! "One can't create the seventh steed of the Sun-God's chariot by harnessing a million hares!"* Anyway, no point explaining it to Thamma. She would not be able to perceive the deep pain that a broken relationship could inflict and might even say, "Don't be upset because the lawyer has tried to prove that you were a 'fallen woman'. In ancient India 'fallen women' were considered to be different and apart from the rest. You too are special, aren't you?"

Jhinuk put her head between her knees. The sole oasis she had in this vast, blazing desert was drying up in the smouldering fire of desperate, indignant anger born of long-drawn repression!

"You don't fit in anymore Thamma, not in my account of things," Jhinuk muttered in a tired voice.

"That's where your fault lies, dear. You can't fit in every little thing in your large calculations about life. You see, the human

---

*Myth has it that the Sun-God Surya drove a chariot with seven horses.

mind doesn't go by logic and reason at all times. It remains outside the parameters of calculated actions. So, one has to make small allowances for it. Look at Sharat for instance, someone who loves fitting people into a fixed scheme. The poor man has failed to fit his wife anywhere."

"Do you know about his wife?" Jhinuk enquired coldly.

Mrinalini nodded. "Sharat thought that his wife should be guarded from public humiliation and protected from the police and court. So, he decided not to proceed with the rape case. But his wife set herself on fire in complete disgust of her cowardly husband. She had expected him to avenge the crime. Sharat never quite realized the woman's sentiments – the support she needed to overcome her shame. The poor man is now suffering from a deep pang of conscience."

Jhinuk's heart stopped beating for a second. Was it some kind of atonement then? A desperate attempt on Sharat's part to clear his conscience? The face of the woman in the court came back to her in a lightning flash. Her child slung across her breast. Sharat had fought for the wronged woman and won the case. But he had to face her wrath as a consequence. Poor man! His plans and efforts were always blown to the winds! Yet he continued to try.

Mrinalini touched Jhinuk on the shoulder. "What is it dear? What are you thinking of?"

"Nothing in particular."

"I won't insist, dear. But you must keep your cool."

Jhinuk stood up. "I refuse to hang upside down and lick honey all my life like the brahmin in your story, Thamma. That's hardly my view of life. That's just a myth."

Mrinalini pulled at Jhinuk's hand, "Forgive the boy, darling. You'll feel better after that, I'm sure."

There was a cloudburst in Jhinuk's heart. "No, never," she cried. "I simply can't Thamma."

"Why can't you? Women have always prevented society from falling apart. It's their inborn ability to forgive that enables them to keep life moving forward. And forgiveness is a noble quality. It empowers you."

Jhinuk threw herself into Mrinalini's lap like a felled tree. "Tunir can go to hell. I'll never look at him again. I don't want to see him ever!"

The rains came once again that autumn evening – in Jhinuk's eyes.

Chapter
Seventeen

*T*he day broke, slowly. Dawn revealed itself, tearing apart a cold curtain of fog. It was a quiet, cool solitude. As the sun rose, the pale colourless sky turned a deep vitriol blue. The young sun smiled benignly. The snow-covered peak gleamed in the sunlight like a work of art.

Jhinuk had climbed fairly high up the winding mountain roads of Gangtok. She stood awestruck, staring unblinkingly at the changing colours of the peaks. They turned from a coal black to a smoky blue. And then to a misty green. The smoky pallor was soon smudged off to reveal a long procession of changing hues...shades of green, brown and yellow. Tears welled up in Jhinuk's eyes. The earth was such a wonderful place! So enchanting, so pretty!

She began climbing down with slow steps. She was going back.

Well-wrapped in jeans, a thick leather jacket, fur cap buttoned at the neck, feet snug in thick woollen socks and shoes, still Jhinuk had little respite from the biting cold of December in the hills. Gusts of freezing wind pierced her body with its sharp nails. She dug her gloved hands deep into her pockets. Even on this freezing December morning, a group of children were on their way to school, clad in bright red uniforms. They went babbling downhill, like a splurging mountain spring, breaking the quiet of the hills. Jhinuk felt slightly nostalgic. Were the morning bells now ringing at Vikramshila Mahavihar too? Two young Lepcha women trudged uphill, loaded with bundles of fresh jungle grass. They turned round to watch the well-dressed Jhinuk walk past them. She walked alone, swaying in rhythm with her motion.

Jhinuk got her breath back after reaching the hotel. A Nepali boy sat nodding in the deserted lobby, the result of last night's hangover perhaps! He managed to answer Jhinuk, after she made several futile attempts to wake him up.

"Tea," ordered Jhinuk, "room 203."

She climbed the carpeted stairway to the first floor, taking off her cap once inside the room, as well as the leather jacket. Hard as it tried, the freezing chill outside couldn't enter this room with all its windows tightly shut. The logs in the fireplace had died down, after crackling all night, their warmth lingering in all corners of the room. It lay trapped within the soft folds of the double bed. It stretched out across the dressing table. The wardrobe. The table and the chairs.

Tunir was fast asleep in the middle of the bed. Curled up and warm. Snug under two thick quilts. They had reached Gangtok only the evening before. Having left for the honeymoon immediately after the wedding, Tunir hadn't fully recovered from the stress and the strain of the last few weeks.

Jhinuk drew the heavy curtains at the window with a noisy jangle. Milk white peaks sparkled beyond the glass panes. The huge mountains were unbelievably near! They seemed to loom right behind the backdoor balcony. Jhinuk stared at the peaks wonderstruck, an eerie feeling running down her body. She rushed up to Tunir, "Hey, how can you sleep so late! Get up! Look outside and see how wonderful the Kanchanjungha looks! It's almost here, within arm's reach!"

Tunir stuck his head out of the quilt and immediately went back to its warm folds. "Um...m...m," he muttered.

"How can you be so abominably lazy? Get up. Don't miss this beautiful scene."

A hand emerged from under the quilt and grabbed Jhinuk. "How did you manage to go out in this awful cold?"

"You don't feel the cold once you're out. I tried waking you, but you wouldn't get up."

"Where's tea? Have you ordered it?"

"I have, dear Sir, I have! Come on, let's go for a walk after tea. Must you laze in bed so late when you're out on a holiday?"

"Well, I haven't come here to go for walks and trips!" Saying this, Tunir dragged Jhinuk under his quilt, and put his arms around her.

Jhinuk tried pleading softly, "They'll serve tea any minute..."

"So what? This is supposed to be a honeymoon suite. Disturbance not permitted."

He smothered Jhinuk with passionate caresses, planting warm kisses on her face, throat, neck and breasts. All coverings were removed, one by one. Here was man, delirious with the mysteries and the cloying sweetness of new-found feminine charm. The soft, fleeting fragrance of fresh young sal flowers had given way to the warm, heady scent of a woman in full bloom. The smell lingered at his nostrils.

"I would have died without you. Simply perished."

Jhinuk drew in the scent of her beloved man. "You would?"

"I had told Didi how I craved for you; longed to be with you. I would have committed suicide if I hadn't got you."

Jhinuk didn't answer. She quietly nestled into the warmth of Tunir's bare body.

Tunir's voice was thick with desire, "Why did you increase my tension by kicking up a silly fuss?"

Jhinuk pressed her lips to Tunir's. A tingling ache rose from somewhere deep down her heart. Couldn't she possibly keep her thoughts free of the city that lay hundreds of miles away?

Tunir rubbed his cheeks fervently against Jhinuk's. "We're silly, aren't we? Strangers like Romita-Palash — people we know nothing about — and some ruffians surfacing from nowhere, and we promptly pick up a silly fight between ourselves!"

The coconut tree of her dreams swayed tall in the darkness of the quilt. It swayed for a few minutes before slowly vanishing from her mind's eye. It would be back. It would certainly return, again and again. Till death came and blinded her.

Even with her beloved so close to her heart, Jhinuk felt completely drained and exhausted for a few moments. The Kanchanjunga across the window lay heavy on her heart. A deep sigh, weighing a few thousand kilograms, struggled to be free of her pulsating lungs. It flung itself against Tunir's face. Dense. And burning hot.

Tunir plunged deeper into Jhinuk's body with an even stronger thirst for union.

Men have never fathomed that sigh. They have never known the amount of hurt, humiliation and pain that women hid within the depths of their hearts to go on loving. It has been like this down the ages.

Palash didn't know. Tunir too would never know.